MEET THE Trash

The Interns

CHELSEA—A brainy **Alicia Silverstone** type with a southern twang, she's shocked by the tell-all topics of *Trash*. But by summer's end, *Trash* could be telling Chelsea's big secret!

KARMA—This Asian beauty is a downtown Manhattan diva with **Fran Drescher**'s voice. Late nights? Cool clubs? Great shopping? Money to be made? Call Karma!

LISHA—Oh-so-cool, hotter than **Demi Moore,** they call her "Luscious Lisha" on the *Trash* set. She's not the same fat, awkward girl that Chelsea grew up with . . . is she?

SKY—Sweet, laid back, a T-shirt and jeans kind of guy who's a whiz with a movie camera, he gets mistaken a lot on the street for **Keanu Reeves** and is everybody's best bud.

ALAN—This sensitive writer from Texas is sure the trash on *Trash* will give him tons of material. If **Johnny Depp** were a writer, he'd be Alan!

NICK—A Canadian slacker with a heart of gold. Chelsea's madly in love with this **Brad Pitt** double, but she has to wait in line behind their famous boss, Jazz Stewart!

continued . . .

The Bosses

JAZZ—The gorgeous **Daryl Hannah**-ish host of *Trash* is afraid of nothing, whether it's posing for nude pix on the beach in France, riding her Harley onto the set while clad in a bikini, or having three boyfriends at once. Because it's all *Trash,* isn't it?

ROXANNE—The beautiful, icy, and ambitious associate producer, she's **Sharon Stone** at age twenty-something and loathes all interns on principle! Behind her back, they call her "Bigfoot" . . . after those gigantic size-twelve dawgs!

BARRY—The slick producer with the power, he's willing to help Chelsea go big places at *Trash.* The question is, is she willing to pay his price?

SUMTIMES—Can a girl have a shaved head and still be gorgeous? Yes! The interns' fave producer got her nickname because she sometimes calls herself Cindy, sometimes Julia, sometimes *whatever*!

TRASH: it's not just a job, it's an adventure!

TRASH

good girls, bad boys

Cherie Bennett
and
Jeff Gottesfeld

BERKLEY BOOKS, NEW YORK

TRASH: GOOD GIRLS, BAD BOYS

A Berkley Book / published by arrangement with
the authors

PRINTING HISTORY
Berkley edition / July 1997

All rights reserved.
Copyright © 1997 by Cherie Bennett and Jeff Gottesfeld.
This book may not be reproduced in whole or in part,
by mimeograph or any other means, without permission.
For information address: The Berkley Publishing Group,
200 Madison Avenue, New York, New York 10016.

The Putnam Berkley World Wide Web site address is
http://www.berkley.com

ISBN: 0-425-15937-X

BERKLEY®
Berkley Books are published by The Berkley Publishing Group,
200 Madison Avenue, New York, New York 10016.
BERKLEY and the "B" design
are trademarks belonging to Berkley Publishing Corporation.

PRINTED IN THE UNITED STATES OF AMERICA

10 9 8 7 6 5 4 3 2 1

For the Wintons,
who know the true meaning
of friendship and family
—David, Suzanne, Sarah, Eric . . .
and Studly.

good girls, bad boys

"I'm inviting you in, in the nicest way I know how," Harley said, pointing his gun at Lisha's head. He kicked the door to the apartment closed with the blunt heel of his motorcycle boot. "Long time no see, baby."

"You know him?" Demetrius asked Lisha incredulously.

"Yeah," Lisha said. "Demetrius, Karma . . . this is Harley."

Harley smiled, and shook the dark, shaggy hair out of his intense blue eyes. "Why don't we all sit down?" He kept his gun trained on Lisha, and she slowly sat in the nearest chair. Karma and Demetrius sat cautiously on the couch.

Harley sauntered around the living room of the Upper West Side Manhattan apartment that Lisha shared with her two best friends, Karma Kushner and Chelsea Jennings.

"Nice digs, huh?" Harley said, turning his head sideways to check out a painting on the wall, representing a piano balanced on nude female legs.

I can't believe this is happening, Lisha thought, her heart thudding painfully in her chest. *I can't believe he broke into my apartment and he has a gun.*

And I know he's capable of using it.

Images flitted quickly through her mind—of Harley and her in London, of falling in love with him, of how it had all gone so very wrong. . . .

"Harley, what do you want?" Lisha asked, careful to keep her voice low and neutral so she didn't betray the abject terror she was feeling.

Harley turned to her. "Hey, is that any way to greet me?"

"Look, whoever you are—"

"Harley," Harley spat.

"Harley," Demetrius repeated. "You really need to put that gun away."

Lisha snuck a look over at Demetrius. Even seated, at six feet four inches of golden, muscular perfection, he was an intimidating sight. Sitting next to him, tiny Karma looked like a lost child.

"Oh, I need to put the gun away?" Harley echoed innocently. "Now, lemme ask you a question, big man, whoever you are. I have the gun. And you have zip. So who gives the orders in this room?"

Silence.

Harley strolled over to Demetrius and jammed the revolver into his right temple. "I said," he began calmly, and then he screamed, *"Who gives the orders in this room?"*

"You do," Demetrius said quietly.

"Oh, much better," Harley replied cheerfully. He moved the gun from Demetrius's temple and went to lounge against the far wall, keeping the pistol trained on Demetrius. "I'm really hurt that you didn't tell him about me, Lish."

"Look, Harley, it's me you have the problem with," Lisha managed. She could hear her voice quavering. "Why don't you just let them leave—"

"No, no, I like a good party," Harley said. He marched over to Lisha and knelt in front of her. "Did you miss me?"

His gun shifted, so it was pointing straight up at her face.

"Wha-what we had was a long time ago, Harley . . ." Lisha began.

Harley's eyes glittered weirdly, staring up at her. "You look really beautiful, Lisha. Hot. And I know you still love me, Lish. Why won't you admit it?"

My God, he's crazy, Lisha realized. *And I think he's high on something, too.*

"You know I care about you," she lied carefully.

"I knew it," Harley said. "All that tough-girl talk over the phone was a big act. I told you I'd find you, Lisha. Remember?"

She closed her eyes, and her last conversation with Harley, in London, flew into her mind. *"It's all over,"* she had told him. *"I don't want any part of you, or your life. Just pretend you never even knew me."*

"But, Lisha," he had told her, *"don't you know it will never be over? You're mine, and it doesn't end*

3

unless I say it ends. I'll find you, wherever you go. Bet on it."

Lisha opened her eyes, and found Harley's eyes glaring into her own. "I remember," she said.

"I went to a lot of trouble to find you, you know," Harley continued. "The FBI is after me—ain't that a kick? I risked my life to come here. You need to thank me."

"Thank you," Lisha managed through tense lips.

"You're welcome," Harley said.

At that moment a siren began to wail on the street, and Harley ran to the window and looked out. "It isn't safe here," he mumbled.

Lisha looked over at Demetrius, who seemed ready to spring off the couch to tackle Harley. She shook her head no as frantically as she could. *He'll kill you,* she mouthed.

Harley turned away from the window and strode over to Lisha. He grabbed her left forearm and jerked her from her chair. His face was inches from hers. "It isn't safe here," he repeated. "I have to leave you now."

Thank God, Lisha thought.

"All right," she said.

"I'll be back," Harley promised. "You know I always keep my promises, right, Lish?"

"Right."

"Will you kiss me good-bye?" he asked, as innocent and hopeful as a starry-eyed suitor.

Hiding her disgust and fear, she leaned forward and kissed him.

"Ah, Lisha, we had it all, remember? I was the

4

only one who saw how beautiful you really were, when no one else could see it, remember?"

She nodded at him all but imperceptibly.

"We can have it all again, Lish," he continued. "I'll be back for you, baby. We'll run away together and leave all this crap behind us, you know? Won't that be great?"

"Great," Lisha agreed, her entire body vibrating with fear.

"Hey, nice to meet you," Harley told Demetrius and Karma, as if they had just hung out together at a really fun party. He turned back to Lisha.

"I know you won't go to the police about this. Right?"

"Right," she echoed.

"Because if the police knew what I know, you'd have to leave this nice apartment and these nice friends behind. And we couldn't be together, which really would be a crime, you know?"

Lisha tried to smile at him.

He kissed her again. "We're forever," he whispered to her. "Just remember, Lish, if I can't have you, no one can."

Then he strode across the living room, pulled open the door, and left.

"Oh, my gawd!" Karma exclaimed in her nasal, New York voice. "What just happened?"

Demetrius was already on his feet, reaching for the portable phone on the coffee table.

"What are you doing?" Lisha cried.

"Calling 9-1-1," Demetrius said, punching the

numbers into the phone. "They can still catch him if they get here fast—"

"No!" Lisha cried, and grabbed the phone out of his hands.

"Are you insane?" Demetrius asked. "That guy is a crazed maniac with—"

"Please, you can't call," Lisha said. She held the phone behind her back.

"But, Lisha, he's really dangerous," Karma protested. "We have to do something—"

"You don't understand—" Lisha began.

"I understand that a pyscho-killer is on the loose!" Demetrius yelled. "Now give me the phone!"

"Please, I'm begging you," Lisha said, tears in her eyes.

The door to the apartment swung open, and Karma actually screamed out loud in fright.

But it wasn't Harley. It was Chelsea, their third roommate, returning from her boyfriend Nick's apartment, across the hall. "Hey, I came to tell you guys there's a great old movie on—"

Then she noticed their faces. "What happened?"

Karma rushed over to the door of the apartment and quickly locked all the locks. Not that those same locks had kept Harley out before, but it still made her feel safer. She turned back to Chelsea. "You know that psycho dude who keeps calling Lisha?" she asked.

"Harley," Chelsea said.

"Right," Karma said. "Well, we just met him, up close and personal. And he has a gun."

Chelsea went to Lisha. "Harley was here?"

Lisha nodded. "He broke in. He had a gun." She fell into the chair and buried her face in her hands. "Oh God, it was so awful. I was so scared."

"And now for some reason Lisha doesn't want us to call the police," Demetrius said with disgust.

"Something happened between Harley and Lisha in Europe," Chelsea said slowly, sitting on the arm-rest of the couch. "Something bad."

Demetrius threw his hands in the air. "What does that have to do with protecting a psychotic, drugged-out—"

"I'm not protecting him," Lisha said, lifting her tear-stained face from her hands. "I'm protecting myself."

Chelsea, Karma, and Demetrius just stared at her, waiting.

I have to tell them the truth, Lisha realized. *I owe them that now. Even if they hate me. Even if I hate myself.*

Lisha took a deep breath. "Here's what happened. I graduated from high school in Colorado a year early," she began, "and then my parents treated me to a trip to Europe. I was only supposed to stay for a month, but I stayed for seven. It completely changed my life." She smiled shakily. "You remember, Chels, what a little butterball I used to be—"

Chelsea, who had gone to grade school with her back in Nashville, before Lisha and her family moved to Colorado, nodded. "But you were still cute, Lisha—"

7

"No, I wasn't cute," Lisha said. "I was fat. And ugly. And that's how I looked when I arrived in London, too. Can you imagine—this fat, naive, little geek on her own in London? I was so pitiful! Well, fortunately, I had a friend who had a friend who kind of took me under her wing—maybe she thought I made her look good, I don't know. Anyway, she got me invited to this party for Crash— they were the hottest new band in London last year. I was scared to go—imagine fat little Alyssa Bishop at this hip rock party with these famous people?

"Anyway, I forced myself to go," she continued. "And I was standing there at that party, all by myself, feeling sorry for fat, little me, when Harley came up to me and started talking. Here was this gorgeous American guy who played the guitar in a band, he told me, and he knew all the guys in Crash, and he's paying attention to me! To *me!* I couldn't believe it.

"That first night, Harley introduced me to speed. He said I'd be able to lose weight without even trying, and I'd have all this energy. And I wanted to please him, and I did want to lose weight, so I took it, and—"

"Lisha—" Chelsea interrupted.

"No, let me finish, or I'll lose my nerve," Lisha said, shaking her bangs out of her eyes. "I did lose weight, more and more weight, and Harley became my boyfriend," she continued. "By this time I was addicted to his little pills. And I guess I was addicted to Harley, too.

"I knew it was bad, I knew I should stop, that I

8

should just leave him and the drugs and get far away from the whole scene. But . . . but I couldn't. For a long time. I mean, I was finally thin. And cute. And . . . I thought I loved him.

"But one day I woke up and I said to myself, 'I can't do this anymore.' So I decided to go visit some friends I'd met who were in Paris. I told Harley we were through, that I wasn't coming back. You see, by that time I had found out that he didn't really make his living with his band, he made his living dealing drugs. I should have known, but I didn't. I was so stupid and blind."

Tears came to Lisha's eyes and she fisted them away quickly, gulping down the lump rising in her throat. "So Harley asked me to take a suitcase of clothes to a friend of his in Paris—American-made clothes, he said, that cost a mint in Paris. And . . . and I agreed. I don't know why—maybe I thought I still loved him or something sick like that. It was only later that I found out there were drugs under the clothes—"

"Oh, Lish—" Karma began.

"There's more," Lisha said. "Harley's drug-dealing partner got busted in Los Angeles. And to make the courts go easier on him, he went and turned state's evidence and told them all the dirt on Harley. So now Harley is wanted by the FBI. But if he's caught, he'll tell them that I transported drugs from one country to another. Don't you see? My entire life will be ruined!"

"But, Lisha," Chelsea said, "you can tell them

9

that you didn't know there were any drugs in that suitcase—"

"They won't believe me," Lisha interrupted. "Everyone knew Harley and I were a couple. And I . . . I knew he was a drug dealer." Tears filled her eyes. "I know you all hate me now—"

"Lisha, we don't," Karma said firmly. "I mean, I could live without your psycho ex-boyfriend threatening my life, but I don't hate you."

"I'm sorry, Lisha," Demetrius said, "but I still think you need to go to the cops. Harley is still out there. He's clearly got some sicko thing for you. What are you going to do, be scared forever?"

"I won't let him ruin everything in my life!" Lisha cried. "I had to get myself off of speed. And I did it! I came home, and got my life together, and now I have this great job as an intern at *Trash*. I want to have a life, and I just want to put Harley and everything that happened in Europe far behind me! Can't you get that?"

Everyone in the living room was quiet as they all thought about what Lisha had just said.

"I do get that," Demetrius finally told her. "I don't think you came to the best conclusion, but I understand."

"Thank you," Lisha said gratefully.

"How about if we all agree not to do anything for tonight," Karma suggested. "But I think you should talk to a lawyer about this, actually."

"A criminal lawyer," Chelsea added.

"You're right," Lisha said. "I will."

"And you'll do whatever the lawyer tells you to do?" Demetrius asked.

"I will," Lisha agreed. "Listen, thanks. I . . . I never wanted to tell you all of this. And I sure didn't want you guys dragged into it."

Chelsea crossed the room and gave her a hug. "You were my best friend when I was a little girl. And you're my best friend now, Lish."

"Hey, what about me?" Karma asked, and she went over to them, too. "Excuse me for a moment of heartwarming girl-bonding," she told her boyfriend, Demetrius, over her shoulder.

"Bond away," Demetrius said. "I'm going to the bathroom. Excuse me." He left the room.

Karma hugged Lisha. "It's not like all three of us don't have problems and secrets, right?"

"Not like mine," Lisha said, laughing shakily.

"Well, I suppose being a Korean girl adopted by Jewish hippies isn't quite as scandalous," Karma conceded. "But then there's the fact that I just found out that I have an identical twin sister I never even knew existed. At least I think she's my sister. That's pretty out there!"

"And then there's my life," Chelsea added. "You have to admit, it's not exactly normal."

That's true, Lisha thought. *Even though Chelsea looks and acts like the most normal girl in the world, her father was actually a mass murderer. He shot and killed a restaurant full of people, then came home to kill his wife and child, meaning Chelsea—but his wife killed him first. And no one knows that terrible secret except Chelsea's mom, me, and Karma.*

"I guess the three of us really *are* in this together, huh?" Lisha said.

"Huh is right," Karma replied. "And I have only one thing to add."

"What?" Lisha asked.

"If ever there were three girls perfect to be interns for the world's trashiest teen TV talk show," Karma said, "it sure is us!"

Lisha lay in bed, staring up at the ceiling, which was, as it always is at night in New York, illuminated by the lights from the street.

No window blinds can keep it all out, Lisha thought idly. *Not in New York City.*

She could hear someone outside singing drunkenly, the sound of distant car horns, and the traffic on West End Avenue. She couldn't sleep.

I can't believe what happened tonight, she thought with a shudder. *Harley really was here. With a gun. And I finally told Chelsea and Karma the truth about what happened to me in Europe. I trust them to keep my secret, but what about Demetrius? He seems really nice, but I hardly know him! He's Karma's boyfriend, and I never would have bared my soul to him like that if he hadn't been held at gunpoint by my ex-boyfriend.*

My ex-boyfriend. Who is stalking me. Who told me he'd be back.

She turned over and tried to get comfortable. The

luminous numbers of the digital clock on her night-stand read 4:01 A.M.

And I have to wake up at seven-thirty to get to work on time, Lisha thought, beating her pillow into a better position.

Trash. *I really and truly work at* Trash, she thought. *It's only the most popular talk show on TV, hosted by none other than nineteen-year-old-ultrahot-gorgeous Jazz, who claims to be the daughter of Rod Stewart.*

Thousands of eighteen-year-olds from all over the country entered the contest to pick six summer interns for Trash, *and I actually got picked. Of course, it probably helped that Jerry Hall, Mick Jagger's supermodel wife, wrote me that letter of recommendation. She was so nice to me when I met her in London. After I got thin, we both modeled in that Rockers for AIDS Research fashion show. I was afraid she wouldn't even answer my letter when I wrote and asked for a recommendation, but she did it right away. And I'd only met Mick and her once before.*

And now here I am, living with Karma and Chelsea. We couldn't possibly be any more different from each other. Karma is tiny, with delicate Asian features, and long, gorgeous hair, and she's the world's greatest expert at mixing designer fashions with thrift-store chic. She's also a whiz at the stock market, and she sounds just like Fran Drescher on The Nanny—*strange combination!*

And then there's Chelsea, who has the biggest, darkest secret of all. You'd never know to look at

*her. With her cute, blond, Alicia Silverstone looks
and preppie outfits, you'd never dream about her
bizarre past. She was even valedictorian of her high
school! How normal can a girl with such a totally
abnormal past get?*

*And me. Karma insists I look and sound like a
young Demi Moore. I sure didn't look like Demi
Moore when I was fat. I can't get fat again. I just
can't. I bet Sky wouldn't be so crazy about me if I
still looked like the old me.*

Sky. He was one of the three eighteen-year-old
guy interns who lived right across the hall from
them. Another was Alan Van Kleef, from Texas. A
romantic, sweet, sensitive guy who wanted to be a
writer, he looked kind of like Johnny Depp. Their
other roommate was Nick Shaw, who was hot and
heavy with Chelsea, a Canadian guy with a slacker
kind of attitude, who looked a lot like Brad Pitt.

And Sky, Lisha thought, *looks just like Keanu
Reeves. Only better. And I want him so much.*

Only no one knows it.

*And no one is going to find out how much I want
Sky, either. Not Chelsea, not Karma, and certainly
not Sky. Because I wanted Harley that much once.
And look what happened.*

No, I'm never going to let Sky know how I feel.

*And right now I have to concentrate on finding a
way of getting Harley out of my life forever. There
has to be another way, other than going to a lawyer.
A lawyer will probably just tell me I should turn myself in, throw myself on the mercy of the court, or
something. My entire life will be ruined.*

14

No, there's got to be another way.

Because I know Harley isn't through with me. And I know he'll be back.

And the next time he shows up with a gun, he might really use it.

"**H**ey, Jazz, wow, I can't believe I'm talking to you!" the recorded, young, male-sounding voice exclaimed into Lisha's earphones. "So, listen, I have this idea for a show on bisexuality, right? Like, you'd be blindfolded, see, and a bunch of different people would kiss you, and you'd have to say if each one was a guy or a girl. Pretty cool, huh? And I volunteer to be one of the people who kiss you, for sure! Oh, my name is Linda Carson, and I'm a girl, even though everyone says I sound like a guy. So, call me, okay?"

Lisha moved the earphones off her ears and rubbed them. She had already spent an hour that morning listening and recording the messages left on the 1-900-I'M-TRASH phone line, where people paid two dollars a minute for the privilege of leaving a message for Jazz with their best show idea.

Every day, there were thousands of such calls.

The interns had dubbed Room 401, the message-recording room, Sicko Central, in honor of how truly bizarre some of the phone messages were. They all spent many hours there, transcribing the outrageous messages from the tapes.

"Well, Linda Carson-who-sounds-like-a-guy," Lisha said out loud, "your idea is just trashy enough to appeal to Jazz, but you didn't leave your phone number, so you're outta luck."

"How's it going?" Sky called, sticking his head into the room. He took a sip from the cup of coffee in his hands.

God, he's so gorgeous, she thought, in spite of all her resolve. *I love the way his hair sort of brushes his eyes, and I love the way his arms look with the sleeves of his denim shirt rolled up like that, and—*

Stop it, Lisha, she told herself. *A guy like Sky is big trouble for you, so just forget it.*

"The usual sickos," Lisha said, her voice casual, betraying nothing of how she really felt. "How come I'm the only one in here this morning?"

"Guess you just got lucky," Sky said. He came in and sat at the desk next to her, straddling the chair backward. "They've got me following one of the camera guys out to Brooklyn in an hour. We're filming a convention of teen girls who have all had plastic surgery to look more like Barbie."

"As in the *doll?*" Lisha asked, making a face.

"The same." He took another sip of his coffee. "So, I heard you had company Friday night."

"Gee, word travels fast," Lisha said, her voice low.

"You want to talk about it?"

"Frankly, no," she said. "And I have to get back to transcribing these delightful tapes, so—"

"Lish . . ." Sky put his hand on her arm. "I really want to help—"

She shook off his arm. "I don't need your help, okay?"

He gave her a sweet, crooked smile. "Look, I know you aren't into me—it's a killer, but I got the message. But that doesn't mean we can't be friends, does it?"

If he only knew the truth, Lisha thought. *If he only knew.*

"We can be friends," she told him, her tone cool.

"So, friends help out friends," Sky said. "And I heard the guy who showed up at your apartment was some serious bad news, that he broke in and had a gun and—"

"Look, Sky, I know you mean well," Lisha said stiffly. "But I need to work this out myself."

He stood up. "Okay. Well, if you change your mind—"

"I know where to find you," she finished for him.

"Right," Sky agreed. "See you." He walked out the door.

Lisha looked down at her arm, at the exact spot where Sky had touched her. It still felt warm.

"My dawgs are totally killing me in these shoes," Karma whined, hurrying into the room. She had on one of her only-Karma-would-put-that-together outfits—very expensive zebra-striped cigarette pants by her favorite designer, Todd Oldham, a short, black plastic jacket over a hot-pink-and-tangerine Lycra T-shirt she had found at Woolworth's for ten bucks. Per usual, she wore high heels so she'd seem taller—today's version were hot pink with black polka dots.

Lisha half smiled, thinking of her own clothing choice—today she'd pulled on a pair of hip-slung jeans and a black suede vest with nothing underneath. The tattoo of a broken heart with a dagger was clearly visible on her shoulder.

I don't remember what Chelsea had on when we left this morning, Lisha thought, *but it was undoubtedly some good-girl preppie little outfit. One thing about me and my roommates, we definitely never swap clothes!*

"Slip 'em off and pick up a set of headphones," Lisha suggested.

Karma sat down next to her and eased her feet out of her shoes with a sigh of relief. "So, are we having a blast here at Sicko Central?"

"Oh, sure," Lisha said. "The usual laugh riot."

"Where's Chelsea?" Karma asked. "I thought she was on Sicko detail, too."

"I'm right behind you," Chelsea said, hurrying into the room.

Lisha grinned when she saw Chelsea—she had called it right, since Chelsea had on one of her usual preppie outfits. Today's was beige chinos with a denim shirt and loafers.

"I had to go walk Jazz's monsters." Chelsea rolled her eyes. "Y'all know I am an animal lover, but I truly detest those two creatures."

Jazz, the nineteen-year-old superstar who was the host of *Trash* had two snarling, nasty-tempered dalmatians that the interns had to walk twice daily. Jazz doted on her dogs as if they were children. They often had intestinal problems, which made walking them and cleaning up after them a particularly daunting enterprise. More than once Lisha had been tempted to disobey New York City's pooper-scooper law.

"Hey, I almost forgot," Karma said, reaching into the pocket of her pants, "I asked my broker for the name of a good criminal lawyer, and she recommended this guy." She handed Lisha the piece of paper with the name and number of the lawyer scribbled on it.

"Thanks," Lisha said, sticking it into the pocket of her jeans.

"You will call, won't you?" Karma asked, sitting at the desk next to Lisha. "My broker says he's good—that he's even been on Geraldo's show at night on CNBC."

"I'll take care of it," Lisha promised, shaking her bangs out of her face. "I never wanted to drag you guys into all of this, I told you. It's bad enough that I have to take Harley's abuse."

"Hey, we're your friends," Karma reminded her. "If you can't abuse us, I ask you, who *can* you abuse?"

"Mail call, mail call," a guy said, wheeling a large mail cart into the room. He was medium height, his brown hair cut into a buzz, with a little mustache and beard around his thin lips. He was nice looking, basically, but he was so shy that he wouldn't ever look any of the girls in the eye.

"Hi, Brian," Chelsea said. "Why don't you just put our mail in our offices, like you usually do?"

"Well, I thought I'd do a special delivery and give you all your mail personally," the guy said. "Hi, Lisha," he added, his voice low. His eyes slid over to her, then looked away again.

"Hi, Brian," Lisha said.

"So, uh . . . what's happening?" Brian asked nervously.

"Oh, we're just working," Chelsea replied.

"Uh-huh," Brian said. "You guys are really lucky you got picked to be interns, you know?" He bit at one of his cuticles. "I bet you have fun, you know, hanging out together and everything."

"Sure," Karma said politely.

"Yeah," Brian agreed. His eyes looked everywhere except at them. "I bet you go to the movies together a lot, stuff like that. You know, like on *Friends* on TV."

"Well, we're pretty busy here at work," Chelsea said.

"Oh, yeah," Brian replied. "But you guys like movies and stuff, I bet."

"Sure," Karma said again, trading looks with Lisha.

"Listen, Brian, we really have to get back to work," Lisha told him. "And this really isn't a good place to leave our mail."

"Oh, yeah, okay, cool," Brian said quickly.

"Okay, so I'll see ya." He wheeled his mail cart out ahead of him.

"What was that all about?" Karma asked.

"I think he's got a thing for Lisha," Chelsea explained.

They all knew that Brian Bassinger, nephew of executive producer Barry Bassinger, had been hired the week before for a summer job at *Trash,* thanks to his uncle. Brian was seventeen and about to go into his senior year at some private school in upstate New York. He was the only *Trash* employee who seemed to have a lower status than the interns—although his connections were better.

"You know, I just thought of something," Lisha said slowly. "You know how we've been trying to figure out who took the film out of the Trash-cam. What if it was Brian?"

The Trash-cam was the video camera the interns were secretly using to create an underground film about the dirty dealings and behind-the-scenes trash that really *was Trash.* They had decided to do it when they all realized they couldn't deal with the underhanded sleaziness of the place without doing *something* to keep themselves sane. Sky, whose father was an official in the TV technicians' union, had borrowed a tiny video camera from a friend of his father's, and the interns had been hiding it in the offices of various executives . . . and just letting the camera run. But the week before, when they retrieved the hidden camera from Jazz's office, they had discovered that someone had removed their film.

Which meant that someone had found their camera.

Which meant that they all expected "someone" to go to Jazz and get them all busted any minute.

"Why would Brian take our film?" Chelsea asked.

Lisha shrugged. "How should I know? But didn't you notice how he kept asking us about movies? What if that was his sly way of telling us he found our Trash-cam?"

"I don't know. . . ." Chelsea said doubtfully. "How would he even know it was our camera?"

"Oh yeah, like it would be hard to figure that one out," Karma snorted. "Lisha could be right."

"Well, even if she *is* right," Chelsea said, "what can we do about it? We can't very well ask him."

"How many?" Sumtimes asked, sticking her head in the door.

The girls were used to this question. Sumtimes, known only by her last name, as she changed her first name weekly, was one of their many bosses. They generally thought of her as the most hard-working *Trash* executive. She often barked out her infamous shorthand query of "how many?"—which basically meant how many or how much of whatever they were supposed to be doing had actually been done.

"I've transcribed a half hour of tape so far," Lisha said.

"Gotta get it done, guys," she told them, scratching a mosquito bite on her completely shaved pate.

She was so beautiful that her baldness actually enhanced her beauty.

"We'll get on it," Chelsea assured her, reaching for her headphones.

"Cool," Sumtimes said. "Because this afternoon you guys—"

"Emily, have you seen Jazz this morning?" Winston Manroot, Jazz's to-die-for gorgeous, dreadlocked Jamaican secretary, asked in his sexy, mellifluous voice.

He looks like a movie star, has that sexy accent, and I heard he went to Harvard, Lisha thought as she studied him. *Now, there's another guy any thinking woman should stay far away from.*

"I just saw her in Barry's office," Sumtimes answered. "Why?"

"I paged her and she didn't answer," Winston said. "That obnoxious reporter from Channel I-forget is on her way over to ask Jazz about some kid in Oregon who is on a hunger strike unless he can marry Jazz. She's called three times this morning already."

"I'll go find her," Sumtimes told him. "Tell the guards not to let the reporter in, okay?"

"Yeah-mon," Winston agreed, his voice a sexy, musical singsong. "I got it covered."

Winston and Sumtimes disappeared.

"I guess Sumtimes is Emily Sumtimes this week, huh?" Chelsea asked idly.

"How cute is that Winston dude, I ask you?" Karma put in.

"Hey, I thought you were crazy about Demetrius," Chelsea reminded her.

"I am," Karma agreed happily. "But that doesn't keep me from appreciating beauty in other life-forms, ya know."

"All of which are male," Lisha added.

"Well, yeah," Karma conceded. "What's your point?"

"My point," Lisha said, "is that fine guys are not worth the trouble."

"Come on, Lish," Chelsea said. "They aren't all like Harley."

"Maybe not," Lisha admitted. "But how do you know ahead of time? I mean, I didn't think Harley was . . . well, like he is, until it was too late, and I was already in love with him."

"He's a really bad guy, Lish," Chelsea said.

"In the words of Jazz, big duh, Chels," Lisha said with disgust. *Big duh* was Jazz's favorite expression.

"Every great-looking guy isn't a bad guy, is what I mean," Chelsea explained.

"You never know," Lisha insisted. "They steal your heart, and then you're at their mercy."

"Yeah, but what's the alternative?" Karma asked.

Lisha reached for her headphones. "It's simple, really. All you have to do is become heartless." She put on her headphones. "And then you have no heart for them to steal."

"This could be it," Alan told Lisha as all the interns met outside Sumtimes's office late that afternoon. A memo had gone around to all of them a couple of hours earlier, telling them to meet Sumtimes at her office at four o'clock. Now they sat on the couches and chairs outside Sumtimes's office while her secretary—a gorgeous girl named Shyanne who was half-black and half-Tahitian, kept a watchful eye on them as she typed into her computer.

"Could be what?" Lisha asked.

"The ax," Alan whispered, eyeing Shyanne to make sure she couldn't overhear them. "Why else would all of us interns be called to a meeting?"

"He's right," Chelsea said anxiously. "We aren't important enough to have meetings—all we do is take notes for other people's meetings."

"No way is Sumtimes firing us," Karma insisted. "If we were busted, we'd get called to Jazz's office."

"Maybe we're not important enough for Jazz to even bother with," Alan said.

"Just chill, you guys," Nick said easily. "If Jazz had found out about the Trash-cam, it wouldn't come down like this."

"Don't you ever worry about anything?" Chelsea asked him.

"Not often," he admitted.

"You could be wrong about how Jazz would handle this, you know," Chelsea pointed out.

"I'm not," Nick said. "I know her."

"Yeah, we all know that you *know* her." Chelsea's voice was cold. "You *know* her really, really well."

I guess Chelsea is still ticked off at Nick for

agreeing to be Jazz's date for the Rock of Ages Awards later in the summer, Lisha thought. *And I guess she feels insecure because Nick used to date Jazz. He told Chelsea he never slept with Jazz, though. Not that you can trust a fine guy to tell you the truth. Nick and Chelsea are supposed to be in love with each other, but who knows what he does behind her back?*

Which only proves my point: love stinks.

The intercom on Shyanne's desk buzzed, and she picked up the phone. "Fine," she said, and hung up. She turned to the interns. "You can go in now."

"We might be about to kiss our butts good-bye," Sky whispered as the six of them got up and filed into Sumtimes's office.

"No negative thinking," Karma admonished him, pushing the tiny braid at the front of her hair off her face.

Alan gave her a cynical look. "We who are about to die salute you."

"Sit anywhere," Sumtimes said from behind her desk. She waved them toward her kidney-shaped pink velvet couch and her bright orange chairs. Everyone sat down.

"Okay, interns, listen up." Fiddling with one of the multiple earrings dangling from her left ear, Sumtimes got down to business. "We need to have quite the serious little chitchat. Karma, shut the door."

As Karma complied, she and Lisha traded looks.

A serious chat with the door closed, Lisha thought. *That could be really bad news.*

28

"I guess you all know why you're here." Sumtimes folded her arms.

Lisha got a sinking feeling. The group eyed each other. *Should we just confess?* Lisha wondered. *Would it make any difference?*

"Well? Doesn't anyone have anything to say?" Sumtimes asked.

The silence in the room was deafening.

"Look," Sky finally said. "I'm really the one you should be talking to. They really didn't do anything."

"So it was *you!*" Sumtimes exclaimed.

"Sky, just forget it, man," Nick began. "You can't take all the blame when we all—"

"All of you?" Sumtimes interrupted, her voice incredulous. "The reporter told me it was only *one* of you!"

"What reporter?" Sky asked, obviously confused.

"You're supposed to be telling me that, don't you think?" Sumtimes responded.

"Uh . . . just exactly what are you talking about?" Sky asked carefully.

"The cover story for *Rave* magazine," Sumtimes said. "What did you think I was talking about?"

The interns just stared at her.

"Wait, hold up here." Sumtimes came around her desk. "Didn't one of you give a secret interview to a reporter named Lydia Love from *Rave* magazine?"

The interns all looked at each other blankly, then shook their heads no.

"You guys aren't just saying that because of that clause in your contract that says you can't give interviews about *Trash* without permission, are you?" Sumtimes asked.

"I didn't even know that clause was there," Chelsea admitted.

"I did," Karma said. "I always read the fine print."

"None of us gave an interview," Alan told Sumtimes. "Honest."

"For real?" Sumtimes asked. "Because she said . . ." She let the rest of her statement trail off. Then she laughed. "I can't believe it! That girl out-TRASHed me!"

"Uh, Sumtimes, we aren't exactly following you, here," Karma explained.

"Yeah, yeah, I know," Sumtimes said. "Okay, it's like this. You guys know *Rave*, right? The new one, that is supposed to be the hippest thing happening? Controversy is, like, their middle name. Well, they wanted to do this big cover story on the *Trash* interns—you know—what happened to the six of you since you got picked and all that. Jazz was not too psyched about that—*Rave* hasn't done a story on her yet—and she turned them down. So this reporter from *Rave*, Lydia Love, claimed she got an interview from one of you and that you blew the lid on Jazz and all the secrets of *Trash*. And if we didn't agree to the full story, they would just print what this unnamed intern had told them."

Sumtimes eyed all of them. "And none of you talked to her, for real?"

"This is the first any of us has heard about this at all," Alan assured her.

"So, what were you talking about, then?" Sumtimes asked Sky. "What was it I was supposed to blame you for and not them?"

"Uh, well, uh . . ." Sky stammered.

"The . . . coffee room!" Karma exclaimed. "Sky trashed the coffee room! Yeah, that's it! The guy is a total slob!"

Sumtimes looked dubious. "You thought I was gonna yell at you guys for trashing the coffee room? But the coffee room is always trashed. It's a permanent condition."

"Yeah, and Sky's responsible for it," Karma said firmly.

Sumtimes gave them a jaded look. "When I shaved my head, my brains did not fly off with my hair. Meaning something is up with you guys that I don't know about."

The interns just smiled at her.

Sumtimes sighed. "Okay, we'll drop it. For the moment, anyway. So, back to this thing with *Rave*. None of you spoke to this reporter? Honest?"

"Honest," Chelsea assured her.

"Absolutely," Alan added.

"For some crazy reason, I believe you guys," Sumtimes said. "Well, anyway, Jazz says *Rave* can go ahead with the story now, providing it's her picture that appears on the cover."

"Figures," Nick said with a chuckle.

"Hey, she got where she is because she's really smart, you know," Sumtimes told him.

"And here I thought it was because she's Rod Stewart's love child," Nick said. "She says."

"Whatever," Sumtimes said breezily. "She's a marketing genius. The point is, she gets the cover, you guys do the story. Just don't say anything Jazz wouldn't want you to say, or your collective ass is grass."

She turned around and picked up an embossed card from her desk. *"Rave* is giving a private party tomorrow night at Tunnel of Love. They want all of you interns there. A photographer will be there to take some shots of you."

"What's Tunnel of Love?" Chelsea asked.

"It's that new club in the East Village, right?" Karma said. "Avenue C?"

"Right," Sumtimes confirmed. "It looks just like an abandoned subway station. They hire actors to pose as bums and junkies and stuff. It's supposed to be really out there."

"Gee, *quel* atmosphere," Karma quipped.

"So, how are we supposed to get in?" Lisha asked. "We're underage."

"Like I said, it's a private party," Sumtimes said. "So there won't be any problem." She handed the embossed card to Chelsea. "Here's the invite. I'll be there, too, to kind of make sure everything goes okay." She stuffed her hands deep into the pockets of her lime-green-and-acid-yellow plaid jumpsuit. "Okay, guys, that's it. Scram."

The interns hustled out of the office.

"Well, we just dodged a major bullet," Alan said as they walked by Shyanne's desk.

"I can't believe I almost opened my mouth and spilled everything," Sky said, shaking his head. "Guilt can do a major number on you."

"You would be one sucky double agent, you know," Karma told him.

"I'll be sure to cross that off my list of career choices," Sky replied as they headed for the bank of elevators.

"It's a good thing I've got the night off from Jimi's tomorrow," Karma said. "I wonder what we should wear to this *Rave* thing." She pushed the down button.

"Oh, one more thing, you guys," Sumtimes called to them, sticking her head out of her office. "For tomorrow night? Dress hot."

"Hot?" Chelsea echoed.

"Hot," Sumtimes repeated. She eyed Chelsea's preppie outfit. "Borrow something from one of your roomies, Chelsea."

"But I'd really rather dress like . . . well, like me," Chelsea said.

"This is an order from Jazz," Sumtimes said. "And you know what we say—"

"When Jazz says, 'jump,' we say 'how high?'" Chelsea recited dutifully.

"Good girl," Sumtimes approved, and disappeared back into her office.

"I don't do 'hot,'" Chelsea said, making a face.

"There's a first time for everything, Chels." Lisha put her arm around Chelsea's shoulders.

"Right," Karma agreed. "Tomorrow night, Lisha and I will turn you into a goddess of the night."

"Oh, you guys, one last thing," Sumtimes called, sticking her head out her door again. "Hot, but not too hot," she qualified. "Jazz will be at the party, too, if you know what I mean." She disappeared again.

"I know exactly what that means," Lisha said. "It means whatever we wear, we have to be sure not to outshine Jazz."

"Ha," Chelsea snorted. "*People* named Jazz one of the fifty most beautiful people in the world. I don't exactly think I'm comp for her."

Lisha looked over at Nick, waiting for him to say something, like that he preferred the way Chelsea looked to the way Jazz looked. But Nick didn't say a word.

Well, we'll just see who outshines who tomorrow night, Lisha thought. *I have a feeling that between Karma and me, we can make Chelsea into a vision so hot that it'll scorch Nick Shaw's eyeballs.*

"So, this could be fun tomorrow night, huh?" Sky asked Lisha.

She shrugged.

He cocked his head at her. "What is that, Lish?"

"What's what?"

"That shrug. You do it all the time. What does it mean?"

"Whatever," Lisha said breezily.

"Huh. An enigmatic woman." Sky smiled at her, and moved closer, gazing down into her eyes. "So, if I ask you to dance tomorrow night, will I get more than a shrug as an answer? I mean, if the music was slow, and I held you close, would you move away?"

Lisha pretended to consider for a moment. "Sounds confining," she decided.

"Confining," Sky echoed. He shook his head. "You sure do know how to hurt a guy, Lish."

She smiled and patted him on the back as if he were her brother.

But inside, her heart was talking.

If you only knew, Sky. If you only knew.

"White spandex hot pants and a cropped rayon shirt that shows your navel," Karma mused, considering Chelsea, who stood there in her bra and panties. She handed her a tiny tropical-print shirt. "It's totally you."

It was the next evening, and Lisha and Karma were planning an outfit for Chelsea to wear to the *Rave* party. They were all in Karma's room, which featured a king-size mahogany canopy bed and more bad art on the walls, compliments of the art-student son of the owners of the apartment. Half of Karma's wardrobe was spread out on the oversized Pakistani-print scarf she used as a bedspread.

"It is definitely not me," Chelsea insisted. "Besides, you wear a size two or something. I wear a size eight."

"I have a lot of stretchy clothes," Karma assured

her, grabbing a neon-striped tube dress off of the bed. "How about this?"

"How about not," Chelsea said, pushing the dress away. "I would feel like I was at a costume party."

"Chelsea's idea of dress-up involves something virginal and flowing, with little flowers on it," Lisha teased.

"So what's wrong with that?" Chelsea asked.

"Nothing," Lisha said. "Except that Jazz will be at this party. And so will Nick. And Jazz will have on something outrageous. Compared to that, one of your little floral Miss Nashville numbers just isn't gonna make it."

"I didn't compete in pageants," Chelsea protested. "And I'm not in competition with her."

"Oh, yes, you are," Karma said. "Nick used to date her, right? Nick is going to the Rock of Ages Awards with her, right?"

"I could just kill him for that," Chelsea said. She sat on the bed, her eyes blazing with anger.

"It doesn't mean anything," Karma assured her. "She just needed an escort, and she asked him, and—"

"And he could have said no!" Chelsea exclaimed.

"She's his boss," Karma pointed out. "You don't get to say no to your boss and still keep your job." She tapped one green-polished fingernail against her lips contemplatively. "I have this Betsy Johnson black leather number that will make you look kind of Pamela Anderson-ish in the bosom department—"

"Her breasts are plastic!" Chelsea said, shuddering with disgust. "Why would I want to look like that?"

"Ask millions of men who drool over her for an answer to that question," Lisha said.

"No black leather," Chelsea said firmly. "No cleavage."

"Okay, okay, wait, I've got it," Lisha said. "I'll be right back."

She ran to her room and pushed through the clothes hanging in her closet. "Ah, perfect," she said triumphantly as she plucked a hanger from the back. She hurried back to Karma's room.

"Okay, Chels, this is definitely you," Lisha declared. She handed the hanger to Chelsea.

On the hanger was a pale peach bias-cut satin nightgown, sleeveless and long, fitted around the bust and dipping dangerously low in the back.

"Uh, Lish, this is a nightgown," Chelsea pointed out.

"Only if you wear it at night," Lisha deadpanned.

"Actually, it's very fabulous," Karma said, feeling the material. "Where did you get this?"

"My aunt Margaret," Lisha said. "She was the only cool relative I ever had, and she died from breast cancer last year. She left me all her clothes."

"So why aren't you wearing it?" Chelsea asked Lisha.

"I'm more into my downtown trash-rock phase these days," Lisha said. "Try it on."

Chelsea slipped the gown over her head. "Well?"

"Oh, my gawd," Karma gasped, "you are totally to-die-for, Chels."

"Really?" Chelsea surveyed her image in the mirror on the dresser.

"Really," Lisha confirmed. "You look like Alicia Silverstone at the Academy Awards."

"Yeah, I wish," Chelsea said, but she was smiling at her reflection. "Y'all really think I should wear this?"

"We-all do," Karma insisted. She looked at her watch. "We have to meet the guys in a half hour and I didn't even shower yet!"

"Are y'all really sure—" Chelsea began.

"We're sure, we're sure." Lisha pushed Chelsea toward the door. "Nick is going to totally die when he sees you, and—"

The phone by Karma's bed rang. Lisha was closest, so she picked it up. "Hello?"

"Miss me?" the voice said.

Harley.

Lisha's stomach dropped to her toes.

"What do you want?" she asked carefully.

"That's no way to greet me, Lish," Harley said, his voice low and sexy.

"I was just . . . just on my way out," Lisha said.

"Yeah, I know," Harley said. "You're going to a party at Tunnel of Love. Are you gonna wear something hot, Lish?"

"How did you know that?" Lisha gasped.

"Oh, I have my ways," he said. "Too bad I can't go with you. You're not going there with a guy, are you?"

She didn't answer.

" 'Cuz you know I'd be really, really angry if you

were going with some guy. And you don't want me to get really angry, know what I mean?"

"I . . . I think you should stop calling here," Lisha began, her voice tremulous.

"Hey, are you gonna wear that sexy underwear I love so much?" Harley asked, his voice low and insinuating. "That flimsy little black bra, and the G-string with the—"

Lisha slammed down the phone.

Chelsea and Karma stared at her.

"It was him, wasn't it?" Chelsea guessed.

Lisha nodded yes, too upset to speak.

"You have to call that lawyer, Lisha," Karma said.

Lisha nodded again.

"Don't just nod, do it!" Chelsea cried. "Lish, this guy is dangerous! You can't ignore this, because it doesn't look like he's going to go away!"

"I know," Lisha agreed, her stomach turning with fear.

You're going to a party at Tunnel of Love. Are you gonna wear something hot, Lish?

How did you know where I was going, Harley? How did you know? I'd better not tell Karma and Chelsea. They'll just freak out.

Lisha put her hands on her stomach, suddenly nauseous.

"In the meantime we'll stick really close to you," Karma promised. "We'll get the guys to watch out for you, too."

"Sky won't leave your side," Chelsea added.

You aren't going there with a guy, are you? Be-

cause you know I'd be really, really angry if you were going there with some guy. And you don't want to get me really angry, know what I mean?

He's watching me, Lisha thought. *I don't know how he's doing it, but he's watching me.*

Which means that no one around me is safe.

No one.

"Well, the six of you are looking really terrif," Sumtimes said, greeting them in front of Tunnel of Love. Normally a line of people would be waiting to get in, but tonight a big sign that read PRIVATE PARTY had been posted. The bouncer, a handsome bodybuilder type with a tattoo on his biceps that read DANGEROUS, stood vigil at the front door, which looked like the turnstile of a subway station.

The always fashionable Sumtimes had on black crepe hip-hugger harem pants with a matching bra top, and multiple chains wrapped around her tiny waist. Her bald pate shone with gold glitter, which matched the gold glitter on her cleavage and pierced navel.

Chelsea had on the pale peach gown, and Lisha and Karma looked just as fabulous. Lisha wore a tiny black miniskirt with a sleeveless baby-blue satin shirt that ended just below her bust, and black lace-up thigh-high boots. Karma had on silver lamé bell-bottoms and a tiny red-and-silver shirt covered with huge flowers, which matched the red-and-silver flowers on her purse and high heels.

The guys looked great, too. Nick wore his usual jeans, sneakers, and T-shirt, but over that he had actually managed to scrounge up a black jacket. Sky had on black jeans and a black shirt, and a black tie covered with Looney Tunes cartoon characters, and Alan wore a gorgeous dark green Italian suit and a collarless shirt.

"Glad we meet with your approval," Alan said. "Our mamas always said we clean up nice."

"So, listen," Sumtimes told them, "remember to follow the ground rules at this thing. Meaning, you only say nice things about Jazz and about *Trash*. Got it?"

"Be nice, got it," Karma agreed.

Sumtimes checked her watch. "Jazz should be here any minute. I want all of us to go in together."

Lisha looked nervously up and down the street. *I half expect Harley to pop out from behind some building,* she thought. *Is he watching me right now?*

"You okay?" Karma asked Lisha, her voice low.

"Yeah, sure," Lisha said halfheartedly.

"You should have let us tell the guys that you-know-who called you tonight," Chelsea whispered.

"I don't want to make a big thing out of it," Lisha insisted, still looking up and down the block.

"But it *is* a big thing!" Karma exclaimed. "Look at you! You're a nervous wreck!"

"What are you a nervous wreck about?" Sky asked, overhearing Karma's remark.

"Nothing," Lisha said quickly. "Forget it."

At that moment a limo with dalmatian-print doors pulled up to the curb. They all knew the unique limo belonged to Jazz.

The chauffeur, a hunky African-American guy

whose muscles bulged in his well-fitted uniform, quickly got out of the car and hurried around it to open the door for Jazz.

She stepped out of the car and shook her famous mane of silver-blond hair back off her face. She wore faded jeans with holes in the knees, a man's white T-shirt, under which it was perfectly obvious she wore no bra, and a motorcycle jacket, which fell artfully off her shoulders.

"Trumped," Karma whispered.

"What do you mean?" Chelsea whispered back. "She didn't dress up at all!"

"Exactly," Lisha said. "Now we look like we're trying too hard, and she looks like she's so cool she doesn't have to try at all."

"Jazz!" Sumtimes said, hurrying over to her.

"Hi," Jazz said, cool as always. Her eyes flitted to the interns. "Hi, Nick."

"Hi."

Jazz sauntered over to him. "I came alone, you notice."

"Uh-huh," Nick said, clearly ill at ease.

Jazz took Nick's arm, then she turned to Chelsea. "You don't mind, do you?"

Chelsea's jaw set hard. She didn't say a word.

"Good, I knew you wouldn't," Jazz said. "Let's go in."

Nick shrugged helplessly at Chelsea as the bouncer held open the heavy door that looked just like the door to a subway train.

"I wish I was just about anyplace on the planet except here," Chelsea whispered to Lisha.

"Don't let 'em see you sweat," Lisha advised as they went through the subway-style turnstile. She took one last quick look around before she entered the club.

I'll feel safe inside the club, Lisha thought. *There's no way he could get into this private party.*

Of course, I thought there was no way he could break into my apartment, and he managed to do that.

The group entered the dimly lit club, which had graffiti spray-painted on the walls. A narrow subway car led to a cavernous room, featuring a giant dance floor surrounded by a circular set of subway tracks. The tunnel surrounding it all was lined with subway-type seats, above which were more graffiti-covered walls. Cans of spray paint were available so patrons could add their own graffiti. Various bums and junkie types were staggering around the room, bumping into people.

"Come with me," Jazz told Nick. "I feel like dancing."

As if she was Moses crossing the Red Sea, bodies parted as Jazz led Nick to the dance floor.

"I hate Jazz with every fiber of my being," Chelsea seethed, watching them walk away.

"Can you spare a buck, honey? I'm hungry," a drunken fetid-breathed bum said, sticking his hand in Chelsea's face.

"Are . . . are you an actor or is this for real?" Chelsea asked nervously.

"Chels, they don't let real bums in here," Lisha said patiently.

"Hey, watch who you're calling a bum, honey," the bum slurred.

"He seems so authentic," Chelsea said.

"Why, thank you," the bum said, his face lighting up, all traces of his drunkenness disappearing. "I study at the American Academy of Dramatic Arts!"

"Gang, follow me," Sumtimes ordered. "We're meeting Lydia Love in the private room upstairs."

Sumtimes led them across the dance floor, where bodies moved in slow motion to a steamy ballad by Alanis Morissette. They went down a dark hallway, hearing a tinny recorded voice announce that the subway had lost all power, then up some stairs and into a dimly lit room, decorated with giant pillows, low-slung couches, and tiny ultraviolet lights.

A young woman with long, straight brown hair, a pierced cheek, and a nose ring sat on a huge red velvet pillow, looking bored. With her was a tall, thin bald guy with three cameras slung around his neck.

"Lydia?" Sumtimes said. "I'm Diana Sumtimes."

Lydia got up gracefully. They shook hands. "And this is my photographer, Chase Gaines."

The photographer nodded at Sumtimes. "Love the hair," he declared.

Sumtimes ran her hand over her smooth pate. "Thanks."

"So, you're the lucky guys who got picked to be the *Trash* interns." Lydia looked them over as she spoke.

"Five out of six," Sumtimes said. "The sixth is downstairs dancing with Jazz at the moment."

Lydia raised her eyebrows. "Jazz dances with interns?"

"Sure," Sumtimes said. *Trash* is a very laid-back place. Everyone parties with everyone."

"Yeah, right," Lisha muttered. Karma kicked her, meaning shut up, keeping a bright smile on her face at the same time.

Lydia reached for a small tape recorder that sat on the table next to her. She turned it on and held a microphone up to Lisha's face.

"What do you hate most about *Trash*?" she asked.

From behind her, Lisha could see Sumtimes's face go white.

"Getting up in the morning," Lisha said smoothly. "I'm kind of a night person."

"Oh, yeah, that's *real* interesting," Lydia said sarcastically. She turned to Sky. "What kind of drugs go down at *Trash*?"

"I'm a clean-living kind of guy," Sky replied.

"Uh-huh," Lydia said, making it clear that she didn't believe him. She turned to Karma. "So, who do you have to do to get a promotion at *Trash*?"

"Everyone," Karma said, deadpan. "Yeah, they force us to have sex with each and every employee if we want to have any hope of ever being anything besides a lowly intern."

Lydia smirked. "Can I quote you?"

"She was kidding," Sumtimes said, rushing forward.

"The name is Karma Kushner, and I was kidding," Karma said, leaning into Lydia's microphone.

"I got a more exciting interview from Marla Trump," Lydia said with disgust.

"We're a drug-free, sex-free, hardworking group of crazy kids," Lisha said cheerfully.

"Okay, great interview!" Sumtimes announced eagerly. "How about we move on to the photo session?"

"I'll have lots more questions for all of you later," Lydia promised, turning off her tape recorder.

"Super-goody," Karma whined. "Can't wait."

"They're all yours for the moment, Chase," Lydia told the photographer.

"Cool," he said. "Okay, for the first shot, I want you three girls all hanging off of Stone Pony."

"Who is that?" Chelsea asked.

"And you guys will be wrapped around Torrid Zone," Chase continued, checking something on one of his cameras.

"Is that an area or a person?" Alan asked dubiously.

"It's me," a young woman said, walking over to them. "Hi, I'm Torrid," she said huskily.

Torrid had long, bright red hair, massive fake breasts, and equally massive muscles. She wore a teenie, tiny leopard-print bikini.

"And I'm Stone," a guy said, coming up next to her. He had long black hair and was also a massive wall of muscles, clad only in a tiny leopard-print thong.

"They're bodybuilding strippers," Chase said casually. "We thought they'd be great for our shots."

"What do they have to do with our interns?" Sumtimes asked nervously.

"Nothing," Chase said. "Does that matter?"

"Uh, did you clear this with Jazz?" Sumtimes asked, sweat breaking out on her bald head.

"She doesn't have photo approval for any photos except her own," Chase said. "Okay, girls, go wrap yourself around Stone. Let's have the blonde wrapped around his waist, the Asian wrapped around his legs, and the brunette in his arms."

"No," Lisha said. "And by the way, we have names. Mine's Lisha."

"No?" Chase repeated, incredulous. "What do you mean, no?"

"I mean, I don't want to," Lisha said. "And I'm not going to."

"Me, either," Chelsea agreed. "I would feel like an idiot."

"Yeah, and 'the Asian' agrees," Karma said. "Why don't you just take normal shots of us?"

"Because normal is boring," Chase replied impatiently. "And *Rave* is never boring."

He shook his head with annoyance. "Okay, we'll start with the guys and Torrid. Torrid, can you bench-press one of these guys?"

"Sure," Torrid said.

"Good, here's what we'll do—" Chase began.

"No, *here's* what we'll do," Sky broke in. "We'll go downstairs and dance. You can take pictures of us, or not. Your choice." He turned to his friends. "You guys with me?"

"Absolutely," Lisha said.

"They dance great!" Sumtimes said quickly. "I mean, dancing shots of them would be great—"

"Would be boring," Chase corrected. "If we don't get some cooperation here, I don't know if this article is going to be a go or not."

"Well, that's just a chance we're willing to take," Lisha said. "Let's go, you guys."

The interns headed out of the room.

"Don't worry," Lisha heard Sumtimes say as the group headed for the stairs. "I'll arrange for any kind of shots you want. I just need a chance to talk to them and to Jazz."

"Well, that was stupid in a major way," Sky said with disgust.

"I don't know," Alan said. "Having Torrid bench-press me would have been a unique erotic experience."

Lisha hit him in the shoulder. "You guys are all alike."

"Not true," Alan protested. "We're all different, and you know it. For example, I'm this sensitive poet who hates football and all those manly-man sports, remember?"

"How could we forget, when you keep reminding us?" Sky said good-naturedly. He gently pushed a strand of hair off of Lisha's face. "You did a really cool thing up there, you know."

"So did you."

"So . . . want to dance?" Sky held out his hand to

her. A slow, sexy tune was playing through the sound system.

I would love to be in your arms, Lisha thought. *But I can't. I don't trust myself to resist you. And I don't want Harley coming after you. I'm not worth it.*

"I don't think so," she said.

"Aw, come on," Sky wheedled, holding out his hand. "Would it really be so awful to slow-dance with me?"

"Hey, hey you! Lisha!" a male voice called to Lisha.

For a moment she was rooted to the spot. *The voice sounds like Harley's,* she thought frantically. *But it can't be. I have to run, but where can I—*

"Lisha!"

She gritted her teeth and turned to face him.

But it wasn't Harley. It was Stone Pony. He had put on a pair of jeans over his thong, and thrown on a denim shirt, which was unbuttoned, revealing his perfect, golden, washboard stomach.

"It *is* Lisha, isn't it?" Stone asked.

"Right," she said.

"Sorry about that up there," Stone said. "I mean, that photographer who hired us was kind of rude, I thought."

"Yeah, me, too," Lisha agreed.

"So, let's start over," he suggested. He held out his hand. "I'm Stone Pony. And you are—?"

"Lisha Bishop," Lisha said, shaking his hand. She quickly introduced her friends.

"No one is really named Stone Pony," Karma told him.

"You're right," Stone said, smiling to reveal his perfect, white teeth. "It used to be Stan Poninski. But that didn't exactly cut it in my line of work."

"I see your point," Karma agreed.

"So, you guys are really interns at *Trash*, huh?" Stone said. "I love that show!"

"Thanks," Alan said. "I think."

"Well, it was nice meeting you," Lisha said politely, turning away.

Stone reached for her arm. "Wait a second."

Lisha turned back to him.

Stone grinned at her. "Look, I know this is going to sound like a big line, but it really isn't. The moment I saw you upstairs, I wanted to know you. You're really gorgeous. Would you like to dance?"

"Take a hike, muscle-brain," Sky said. "She doesn't want to dance with you."

"Sky!" Lisha hissed. "Kindly shut up!"

"What?" Sky asked. "You're not going to fall for that I'm-so-honest-and-disarming routine, are you? The guy just wants to get in your pants, Lish!"

"All he did was ask me to dance!" she exclaimed.

"Well, so did I!" Sky fumed. "And you turned me down!"

Lisha narrowed her eyes at Sky, then she whirled around to Stone. "I'd love to dance with you," she declared.

"Great," Stone said. He reached for her hand and led her to the dance floor.

Sky watched as Stone took Lisha into his arms. "I don't believe it," he muttered, his hands clenched into fists.

Lisha looked over at Sky, who just stood there, staring daggers at her. She moved closer to Stone, reached up, and wrapped her arms around his neck.

Then she closed her eyes, and wrapped in Stone's muscular arms, she swayed to the music.

I won't think about Harley, or Sky, or anything at all, she decided. *Sky has a helluva nerve getting all possessive about me. Forget him. Forget complications.*

All I want to feel is the heat of this moment.

And then she moved even closer into Stone's arms.

Honk. Honk. *Honk!*
Honk honk honk honk honk!
All around the Kushners' health-food-store van, a cacophony of auto, truck, and bus horns started blaring. At first there were just a couple, and then other drivers chimed in, and then more and more, until it seemed like all the drivers backed up inside the Queens Midtown Tunnel, waiting to pay their tolls, were leaning on their horn.

"Why do they do that?" Lisha asked from her spot in the backseat of the van. She put her hands over her ears. "It doesn't accomplish anything!"

"New Yorkers love to make a racket," Karma said, throwing her head back against the headrest. "This is endless. We've been sitting in this exact spot for almost two hours!"

Lisha rubbed her temples, where a headache was starting to form. It was the next evening. And somehow Karma had talked Lisha into going with her to talk to her parents about how she, Karma, had actually met a person she strongly suspected was her identical twin sister. Karma had pleaded the need for moral support, and Lisha had said yes.

So Karma had called her parents from work and told them that she wanted to see them—could they pick up her and Lisha and bring them out to the house for dinner? Marty and Wendy were only too happy to oblige.

I guess I was flattered that she asked me instead of asking Chelsea, Lisha thought. *Or maybe I was her second choice, since Chelsea is off doing something or other with Nick. After Jazz made Nick dance with her all night last night, it's going to take some work for him to get back in Chelsea's good graces.*

Lisha looked at her watch and sighed.

"What can I tell you?" Karma said. "When you're stuck, you're stuck."

"Try meditating, girls," Mrs. Kushner suggested good-naturedly from the front seat. "It can do wonders for you."

"Oh, thanks, Mom," Karma whined, rolling her eyes. "That's very helpful."

The plan they had arranged was that they'd drive out to the Kushners' house in Hewlett, Long Island, and then, over dinner, Karma would talk to them about the girl she had met who she was now certain was an identical twin sister that she had not known existed. After that, the Kushners would drop them at the subway near JFK Airport, and they'd ride the A train on its return trip to Manhattan.

The only problem, Lisha thought, looking at her watch again, *was that we were supposed to be at the Kushners' house an hour ago. And an hour from now, we're supposed to be on the subway back to Manhattan.*

"Must be an accident at the other end," Karma's former-hippie father, Marty, replied. "I'll put in another tape, honey." He reached into a box of cassettes that was sitting between him and Karma's mother, Wendy, on the front seat of the car.

Karma looked at Lisha and made a face. "Prepare your virgin ears for a Grateful Dead assault," she warned her friend.

"It's John Tesh," Wendy advised them with a smile as she reached behind her neck to free her waist-length straight gray hair from her seat belt. "Not the Grateful Dead."

"Oh great," Karma quipped. "New Age music to have your blood boil by. A concerto for synthesizers and automobile horns?"

Lisha laughed, even though she was as frustrated as Karma was by the unmoving traffic.

"You'll love it, honey," Marty said to her. He seemed unfazed by the intense traffic backup.

"Yeah, right," Karma groused. "Can't you play something by Smashing Pumpkins or Tori Amos instead?"

Lisha tapped her watch as she looked at Karma, who made a face in return.

She doesn't want to have this conversation with them, Lisha realized. *It's making her really nervous.*

"Just do it," Lisha advised out loud, her voice muffled by the honking car horns.

"I don't want to just do it here," Karma said.

"Putting it off isn't going to change anything," Lisha pointed out.

"Oh, yeah?" was Karma's retort. "If you're so good at doing stuff you dread, why haven't you called that lawyer yet about you-know-what?"

"I'll get to it," Lisha said defensively, "and don't change the subject." She checked her watch again. "Look, your father is going to have to turn around at the tollbooth and take us home anyway, or you'll be late for your shift at Jimi's, and you won't have—"

"What are you two talking about?" Wendy asked conversationally.

"Oh, nothing," Karma said quickly. She smiled at her mother. "Just, you know . . . talking."

Wendy turned around in her seat. "Karma Kushner," she admonished her daughter gently, "I'm your mother. Don't you think I know when you're hiding something?"

"Yeah, and overhearing your conversation didn't hurt, either," Marty added with a grin.

Wendy made a face at her husband, then turned back to Karma. "Spill it, please."

The traffic wasn't moving at all, so Marty Kushner took his eyes off the road and turned around to face his daughter, too.

Lisha couldn't help it. She stared at her friend, too.

What's she going to say? she thought. *And how is she going to say it?*

Karma seemed to shrink in her car seat and appeared even tinier than she really was.

"And so?" Wendy prompted her. "You're about to tell us that you're giving up black coffee and hot dogs forever and becoming a macrobiotic vegetarian?"

"Worse," Karma said meekly.

"Honey," Marty said, his voice full of kindness, "if you haven't been arrested and don't have a fatal disease, there's nothing you can say to us which will throw us. I guarantee it."

"You sure?" Karma said.

"Sure," Marty and Wendy said at the same time.

These two are amazing, Lisha thought. *How come my parents couldn't be more like them?*

"I think . . . well, that is I'm pretty sure that . . . I have a sister," Karma said. "A twin sister. An identical twin sister."

"We know," Marty said.

They what? Lisha asked herself, shocked.

"You *know?*" Karma asked incredulously. "Do you want to run that by me again?"

"We know you think you may have a twin sister," Wendy said.

"But how?" Karma asked. "I never—"

"Look, honey," Marty said. "Ever since you started working at *Trash*, we tape it every day and watch it before we go to bed."

Lisha could see that this statement took a second for Karma to digest.

"You watch *Trash*?" Karma asked.

"I just said that," Marty said. The car behind him gave a couple of quick beeps on the horn, and Marty pulled forward three or four feet in the traffic. Then the wall of cars and trucks stopped again.

"We saw that advertisement that had your picture on it," Wendy said.

"You did?" Karma said dully. "I can't believe you guys watch *Trash*. You are the last two people on the face of the earth that I ever thought would—"

"We watch it because you work there," Wendy said, "and we're your parents. When we saw that ad, we guessed that you thought you had a sister. Why else would you advertise on TV for someone who looks like you?"

"So why don't you explain to us what's going on, exactly?" Marty said. He reached for the volume knob on the van's tape deck, and turned the John Tesh music way down, until it was no more than a hum.

Karma sighed. "I guess I should start at the beginning."

"That would be a good place," Wendy agreed.

Lisha listened, fascinated, as Karma let the story unravel for her parents, beginning with how Demetrius mistook someone for her on the street, going through how she had seen someone who looked just like her on a city bus, and concluding at Jimi's when a girl who looked just like her, whose name Karma found out later was Janelle Cho, came into the club and ordered a drink from Karma.

As she talked, Lisha recalled how Karma, after she'd been convinced that there was another girl in New York City who looked just like her, had convinced the powers that be at *Trash* to run a short advertisement on the show featuring Karma's picture, and asking anyone who thought they looked like her to contact *Trash* immediately.

We got thousands of photos, Lisha thought. *And most of them didn't look like Karma at all. In fact, that had nothing, finally, to do with how Karma found Janelle!*

When Karma finished, fifteen minutes had passed, and the traffic had moved forward a bare two hundred yards.

"So, that's it," Karma concluded. "Except for the fact that when Janelle and I had coffee together, she told me she doesn't want anything to do with me. She says her life is fine the way it is, and doesn't want any complications. I've called her four times, and left her messages on her machine, but she never calls me back."

"Wow," Wendy said.

"I'll second that," Marty added.

"So if you saw me on *Trash,* with the ad," Karma asked, "how come you didn't say anything to me?"

"We were waiting for you to come to us," Marty explained. "We thought that was the right thing to do."

Cool, Lisha thought. *Very cool. That's the kind of parent I want to be. That is, if I'm ever a parent.*

Which I never will be. Since I plan never to fall in love and get married.

"But if you didn't bring it up by the end of July, we were going to bring it up with you," Wendy added, reaching for a small bottle of mineral water that was perched in the center console, and taking a sip.

Even cooler, Lisha thought.

"So what do you know?" Karma asked them.

"Not much," Marty said. "We adopted you when you were two days old. The adoption agency told us that you didn't have any brothers or sisters, and certainly didn't say anything about a twin."

"That's for sure," Wendy added.

"And I have to admit, it really troubles me. I don't like the idea that they lied to us, or that they separated twin sisters like that."

"Would you . . . would you have adopted both of us, if you'd known I was a twin?" Karma asked hesitantly.

Marty and Wendy traded looks. "I honestly don't know," Wendy finally said.

"Unreal," Karma said. "I mean, if you had known about my twin, you might not have adopted me. And I might never have been your daughter."

"I know this sounds terribly fatalistic," Wendy said, "but I believe you were destined to be our daughter."

"And we can't imagine life without you," Marty added.

"The two of you ought to give lessons in how to be terrific parents," Lisha told them.

"Oh, we've made plenty of mistakes, believe me," Marty said. "But thanks for the compliment."

"So, Karma, do you want us to contact the agency again?" Wendy asked.

Karma nodded.

"Don't be disappointed," Marty warned her. "They may not be able to tell us anything."

"Well, they don't have to tell me she's my twin," Karma said, "because I already know that. I sat across the table from her and it was like looking at myself, minus the great fashion sense, of course."

Wendy reached for her daughter's hand. "So, how do you feel about all this?"

"Weird," Karma said.

"Bad," Lisha corrected.

"Okay, weird *and* bad," Karma admitted. "How would you like to find out you had a twin sister who didn't want to have anything to do with you?"

"Give her time, honey," Marty said gently, looking at his daughter through his rearview mirror. "This has to be a shock for her, too. Maybe she'll come around."

"I doubt it," Karma said unhappily. "See, the people who adopted her are Korean, too. And no one knows she's adopted. That's how their whole family wants it."

Wendy patted Karma's hand again. "Well, we'll do everything we can to get you information, sweetie."

"I know," Karma said with a sigh.

Lisha smiled at her friend, and hugged her shoulders. "Hang in there."

Karma gave her a small smile. "Well, Lish, I guess now you know all the family secrets."

"If my family was more like the Kushner family," Lisha said, "there'd be a lot fewer secrets in my parents' house."

Like what happened to me in Europe. My parents don't know a thing. And I could never, ever tell them, she thought.

"We'll be happy to take you as one of our kids," Marty said.

"Yeah, we could be fraternal twins," Karma cracked.

Everyone laughed as the car horns started up again, and within seconds the decibel level in the tunnel was once again completely excruciating.

I can't believe I'm out of shampoo, Lisha thought, as she turned her bottle of Aussie Miracle upside down and watched as nothing dripped out.

It was very late that evening. Marty and Wendy Kushner, had, in fact, turned around and driven Lisha and Karma back to their apartment, when they'd finally gotten out of the Queens Midtown Tunnel, at 9:30 P.M. that night. The holdup had been caused by an actual *holdup* at the toll takers' booth, and the police were conducting a thorough investigation. Karma had hurried off to work, worried that her boss, Arnold, was going to kill her for her tardiness.

Shampoo, shampoo, who uses my brand of shampoo? Lisha thought as she stepped out of the shower. *Not Chelsea and not Karma, and I hate the stuff they use.*

"Alan uses Aussie Miracle," she recalled out loud as she wrapped herself in an oversized terrycloth bathrobe and wrapped a towel around her wet hair.

That's right, she thought. *We laughed together one night over how particular we both are about using that shampoo. I'll go across the hall and borrow some from Alan.*

Lisha stuck her head into the hallway and looked around carefully. *No sign of Harley*, she thought. *I've got to do something about him. I just don't know what.*

She looked down under the door of the guys' apartment and saw some light, so she knew that someone was awake inside. She gave the quadruple code knock they'd all worked out. Then she knocked again.

The door opened.

Alan stood there, clad only in a small towel wrapped around his hips, his hair wet and tousled.

"Hey, Lisha," he said, his voice betraying a slight south-Texas drawl. "What's going on?"

"You look like you just stepped out of the shower," Lisha commented.

"Looks like you did, too." Alan smiled. "Come on in."

Both the girls' and the guys' apartments had been rented fully furnished by *Trash*, and while they were about the same size and layout, they couldn't have looked any more different. The girls' apartment featured overstuffed furniture and bad erotic art, but the guys' apartment was done in industrial chic. Everything in the apartment was made of metal, from the hard-edged frame on the uncomfortable black sofa, to the coffee table made from gray pipes. Sky, who was from Brooklyn, had a buddy of his bring the comfortable BarcaLounger from his family's living room over in his van. The brown easy chair sat incongruously amid the black-and-gray metal furnishings.

"I came to beg some shampoo, actually," Lisha said, stepping into their living room. For a moment she felt keenly aware that Alan had on nothing but a towel, and she had nothing on under her robe. "You use—"

"Aussie Miracle," Alan filled in. "Yeah, I remember you do, too."

"And I'm out," Lisha said.

"No problem," Alan said easily. "I'll get it—"

The phone rang.

"Just a sec," Alan said, snatching up the phone on the metal coffee table. "Hello?"

As he talked into the phone Lisha couldn't help but notice how cute he looked, clad only in a towel, with his hair all wet and tousled.

For someone who doesn't like sports, he sure is in great shape, she thought, checking out his lean and muscular torso. *In fact, he's incredibly cute. Huh. I never think of Alan that way. Maybe it's because he used to have such an intense crush on Chelsea. Or maybe it's because he doesn't come on like a macho man, like Sky. I always just think of him as my bud.*

"Listen, I'm telling you the truth," Alan was saying into the phone. "Yeah, I promise I'll give Nick your message. Yes, word for word. Okay, bye." He hung up the phone.

"One of Nick's admirers?" Lisha asked.

"An ex, I guess," Alan said. "There are many."

"And they still call him here?"

Alan nodded. "His old roommates give them this number. They call all the time."

"Does Chelsea know that?"

"No," Alan said. "I tried to warn her once, that Nick isn't ready for the kind of serious relationship she wants, but—"

"She wouldn't listen," Lisha filled in.

"Something like that," Alan agreed. "Listen, I'm not busting Nick. He's a great guy and I know he really cares about Chelsea. In fact, they're out somewhere together right now. They even took Belch with them."

Belch was Nick's dog, who was famous for his ability to belch on command.

"Is Sky home?" Lisha asked casually.

"He went out for a burger," Alan said. "You know we never have any food in this apartment. So, I'll get my shampoo for you."

"Thanks," Lisha said. She sat on the couch and tried to get comfortable, failed, and got up to plop herself down in the easy chair.

There's some button here that makes this thing vibrate, she recalled, and she fumbled around with the knobs at the bottom of the chair.

She pushed the wrong one. The chair slid backward until the back was practically parallel with the floor, the footrest came up, and Lisha found herself facing the ceiling, her bathrobe all the way up her thighs.

"Hey, man, I brought you back a burger—" Sky said as he came into the apartment.

Lisha fumbled wildly, caught in the chair, trying to adjust her bathrobe and reach for the knob to set her upright at the same time.

"Great outfit," Sky said with a grin.

"Shut up," Lisha snapped, her face blazing with embarrassment. She pulled down her bathrobe.

"You know, I've fantasized about you dressed just about like that, in that chair—" Sky began.

Lisha managed to right the chair, and she stood up. "I don't want to hear about your fantasies, okay?"

"Lish, I'm only kidding," Sky said. "I just meant that I'm glad to see you."

"I just came to borrow some shampoo from Alan," Lisha said stiffly.

"Oh," Sky replied. He set Alan's burger down on the table. "I shouldn't have gotten my hopes up, huh?"

"Right," Lisha agreed.

Sky moved closer to her. "I just . . . I feel this heat between us, you know? You keep denying it, but I keep feeling like it's there."

It is, Lisha thought, barely breathing. *Do you know how much I want to touch you? But it's too dangerous. That kind of passion got me into big trouble before. And I'll never, ever let it happen again.*

"There's nothing there from my point of view," she said coolly.

Sky stood so close to her that she could feel his warm breath on her face, his lips were so close to hers.

"Nothing?" he asked, his voice low.

Now his lips were almost on hers. *It would be so easy to give in. So easy.*

"Sorry I took so long," Alan said as he came back into the room. "I was trying to find a new bottle and it was all the way in the back of my—" He stopped, taking in the sight of Sky and Lisha. "Oops. Guess I'm interrupting."

Lisha jumped away from Sky. "Not at all," she said, her voice a little too loud.

"Lish—" Sky began.

"Forget it," she said quickly.

"Lish, come on—"

Lisha ignored Sky, went over to Alan, and took the shampoo. "Thanks. You're a lifesaver."

"Lisha, come on, stay and we'll talk," Sky said.

"There's nothing to talk about," she said firmly.

And then, before she had a chance to think about it, to prove her point that there was absolutely nothing going on between her and Sky, Lisha leaned over and—to the shock of all three of them—kissed Alan softly on the lips.

Then she turned on her heel and walked out of their apartment, leaving two speechless guys behind her.

"**Y**ou did *what*?" Chelsea asked Lisha.

"I kissed Alan," Lisha said.

It was the next morning, and Chelsea and Lisha were walking to work together. Karma, even though she'd gotten hardly any sleep the night before because of her late shift at the hip teen downtown club, Jimi's, had gone in early to *Trash* to prepare for a meeting. Later that day she was scheduled to see their most hated boss of all, Roxanne Renault—also known as Bigfoot, because of the gigantic size of her feet.

"You and Alan?" Chelsea asked. "I never thought of the two of you together." They sidestepped a street vendor selling knockoff wristwatches and rounded the corner. "How did this happen?"

Lisha explained what had happened the night before. "And then I just . . . I just kissed him," she concluded.

"So wait," Chelsea began, "you're telling me you're not into Sky but you are into Alan?"

"I'm not telling you anything except the facts of what happened," Lisha hedged.

Chelsea looked at her sideways. "Is it possible that you really are into Sky, but you're only pretending not to be?"

"Why would I do that?" Lisha asked nonchalantly.

"I don't know," Chelsea confessed. "I just get this feeling sometimes."

"It makes much more sense for me to be with Alan," Lisha said firmly.

"Why?" Chelsea asked.

"Because chemistry is highly overrated," Lisha declared as they approached the glass doors of the building where *Trash* was taped daily in front of a live audience.

"Oh, so you *do* want Sky—"

"Just forget it," Lisha said quickly. "I'm not looking for any kind of big relationship with anyone."

They walked into the cool, air-conditioned lobby and stood with all the other people waiting for an elevator.

"Did you call that lawyer yet?" Chelsea asked Lisha.

"I've been busy," Lisha said, blowing the bangs out of her eyes.

"You have not," Chelsea accused. "You're just scared to do it."

"I'm not scared," Lisha denied.

72

"Lish, you can't just blow this off, I mean it!" Chelsea exclaimed. "Harley could show up anywhere, at any time, and he's really sick! How about if Karma and I go to see the lawyer with you, would that help?"

"Don't push me, okay?" Lisha said. "I said I'll get to it, and—"

"Hi, how are you, how's it going?" Brian Bassinger said eagerly, sidling over to them. He was holding a pile of manila envelopes, which Lisha recognized as interoffice memos.

"Hi, Brian," Chelsea greeted.

"I got here an hour ago," Brian said. "The early bird gets the worm, Uncle Barry says."

"Great," Lisha managed.

He gazed at her with adoration. "Wow, Lisha, you look really, really nice today."

Lisha looked down at herself. She had on a plain black slip dress, very short, and combat boots. "Thanks, Brian."

"And I love your perfume," he added.

"I'm not wearing perfume, Brian," Lisha said.

"Wow," he repeated, unable to take his eyes from her.

The elevator arrived, and the girls piled in with the rest of the crowd. Brian was wedged right up against Lisha. He stared at her all the way up to the fourth floor.

"Bye, Brian," Lisha said, since he seemed rooted to the spot and unable to move, and blocked her exit from the elevator.

"Oh, yeah, bye," Brian said, and he edged out of the way, letting Lisha and Chelsea pass by.

"That guy has it really bad for you," Chelsea commented as they headed down the hallway toward the tiny cubicles that masqueraded as their offices.

"He's kind of creepy," Lisha said, making a face.

"Oh, he is not," Chelsea replied with a laugh. "He's just crazy about you, that's all."

"Speaking of people who are crazy about people, how was your date with Nick last night?" Lisha asked.

"Great," Chelsea said with a sigh. "And you're right. I *am* crazy about him."

They had reached their offices. Lisha leaned against the wall. "Did he talk about what's going on with Jazz?" she asked.

"No," Chelsea said. "He steered clear of that subject."

"Bummer," Lisha commented.

"Hey, interns!" a female voice barked at them. They turned around. It was Roxanne Renault, a.k.a. Bigfoot. A Sharon Stone look-alike, except with red hair, she limped toward them on crutches, one of her massive feet encased in a cast covered by orange-and-pink silk, which matched the orange-and-pink silk of her minidress.

Bigfoot had recently been shot in the foot by a crazed guest on *Trash*. She was still recovering from her injury, and the interns were bearing the brunt of the wrath her pain induced.

Not that she was a pleasant personality before she was wounded, Lisha thought. *Hardly.*

"Good morning, Roxanne," Chelsea said cheerfully.

"I'm not interested in morning chitchat, okay?" Roxanne snapped. "My foot is killing me and a pipe burst in my office this morning and soaked a bunch of my files. Which means I'm in a bad mood. Get it?"

"Got it," Lisha confirmed.

"Good," Roxanne said. "I expect the two of you at the one o'clock meeting about the Kids of Serial Killers show we're planning."

"I'm not working on that," Lisha reminded her.

"Look, if I say I want you at the meeting, then your butt will be at the meeting, right?"

"Right," Lisha agreed.

"Good answer," Bigfoot said. "And Chutney, go clean up the mess in my office. Bring a squeegee." She hobbled away.

Roxanne called Chelsea Chutney because Chutney was the name by which Jazz had mistakenly referred to her, on the air, after Chelsea had saved Jazz from the crazed gun-toting teenager, Sela Flynn. All Sela had done was taken the entire *Trash* set hostage, Jazz included.

Just another day at the Trash-bin, Lisha thought to herself.

"What a charmer," Chelsea muttered.

"I'd like to shoot her in her other foot," Lisha said.

"Can you imagine if she ever found out the truth about me?" Chelsea asked, shuddering.

She means that mass murderer Charles Kettering is her father, Lisha thought, *and that Bigfoot would love nothing more in this world than to uncover her secret, and expose her in front of the entire world.*

"Bigfoot is not going to find out," Lisha said firmly. "Karma scammed her into believing that Chelsea Kettering lives in Australia and turned down the chance to be on *Trash*, remember?"

"I remember," Chelsea said. "But I always feel like I'm *this* close to getting busted."

"Don't worry," Lisha told her. "Roxanne isn't nearly as smart as she thinks she is. If she wasn't doing the nasty with Barry Bassinger, Executive Producer, I bet she wouldn't even have a job here."

"Maybe," Chelsea said dubiously. "I just get so nervous around her."

Lisha hugged Chelsea. "Karma and I told you we'd keep your secret, and we will, Chels. Not to worry."

"Thanks," Chelsea said gratefully. "So, why is it that you'll help me with my problems but you won't let me help you with yours?"

"I don't need any help!"

"You need to go to see that lawyer—"

"I will—"

"Just call him," Chelsea insisted. "Promise me you'll call him today."

"Boy, you can be a real pit bull when you want to be," Lisha groused.

"A pit bull who cares about you," Chelsea said.

"I guess I'd better go clean up Roxanne's mess."
She sighed. "I'll see you later. Oh, and don't forget
what I said about the lawyer, okay?"

"Yeah, yeah." Lisha waved her off, then went
into her tiny cubicle and sat behind her desk. On top
of a pile of papers sat an envelope, with *Lisha* written on the front.

"What's this," she murmured to herself as she
opened the sealed envelope. A typed note fell out.
She read it quickly.

Dear Lisha,

I can't stop thinking about you. Meet me on
the third floor, in the film storage room, today
at one-thirty. Or else.

The note wasn't signed.

Lisha's hands began to shake.

Harley, she thought. *He got past the guards
downstairs, and he got into my office. He's watching me. He's right here at* Trash.

Oh God . . .

"What should I do?" she whispered out loud to
herself. "Please, I don't know what to do—"

"Hey, you okay? You look like someone died."

It was Alan, sticking his head into the doorway of
her cubicle.

"Oh, sure," she said, her voice shaky. "Fine."

"You don't look fine," Alan said, his voice concerned. He came into the office. "Can I help?"

Lisha stood up and went to him. "If it wouldn't

sound too crazy, you could put your arms around me and hold me," she whispered.

Alan opened his arms, and she moved into the comfort of his embrace. For a long time she just stood there, her eyes closed, feeling momentarily safe.

Safer, anyway.

"Lish, what is it?" he finally asked, his mouth in her hair. "You're shaking—"

"I can't talk about it," she said quickly. She took a step away from him. "But, thanks. You helped."

He gave her a small smile. "I know you can take care of yourself, Lish. But I just want you to know that I'm your friend. And I care about you."

"I know you do, Alan." She walked over to the window and looked down at the street. "Did you ever wish you could just erase your past?"

"I'm afraid my past isn't exciting enough to harbor a wish like that," Alan admitted. "If it was, I'd probably be a lot better writer than I am—you know, you can't write it unless you've lived it, and all that."

"Well, I've lived it," Lisha said, still staring out at the street. "And now I have to pay for it." Her eyes filled with tears until the street scene below was just a blur.

She heard Alan cross the room, and then she felt his hands ever so gently on her shoulders. He turned her around. Then, without saying a word, he took her in his arms again.

This is what I need, Lisha thought. *To feel safe. I'll never feel this way with Sky. He's too danger-*

ous. And I never, ever want to feel that out of control again.

And then she lifted her lips to Alan, and she kissed him. For just a moment he hesitated, and then . . . then, he more than answered the warmth of her kiss with his own.

"Okay, let's review," Bigfoot said, her cast-clad foot, as usual, propped up on her desk. Lisha, Chelsea, and Karma had to lean to one side or the other in order to see Roxanne's face from the other side of her humongous foot.

"Karma, update, Teen Kids of Serial Killers," Bigfoot barked.

Lisha snuck a quick look at her watch. *One o'clock. I'm supposed to meet Harley in the film storage room in a half hour. What should I do? Should I go? By myself? But what if he has a gun? No, he couldn't possibly have snuck a gun past the metal detectors downstairs. But what if I don't meet him? And he goes to the police? My whole life would be ruined and I—*

"Lisha, are you with us?" Roxanne asked.

"Oh, yes, of course," Lisha said, her attention snapping back to the meeting.

"So, what did Karma just say, then?" Bigfoot demanded.

"I, uh . . ." Lisha stammered.

"What is this, junior high?" Roxanne asked. "What is your problem?"

"No problem," Lisha said, trying to sound like her usual cool self. "Continue."

"Oh, I have your permission?" Roxanne sneered. "Karma just gave us short sketches of the three teen kids of serial killers who have already agreed to be on our show. You daydreamed through the whole thing."

"Sorry," Lisha said.

"I brought you into this because I thought you had it together enough to contribute to this show. Jazz expects us to pull incredible ratings with this. I expect your full attention. Got it?"

"Got it," Lisha assured her.

"Yeah, I bet." Roxanne turned to Karma. "Okay, continue. Move on to the Chelsea Kettering recap."

"Okay," Karma said, scanning her notes. "Well, let's see, we wanted to get Chelsea Kettering, but when we spoke to her in Australia, where she's attending college, she absolutely refused to be on the show."

Actually, Bigfoot only thinks she spoke to Chelsea Kettering, Lisha recalled. *The person she really spoke to was some actress in Australia who was pretending to be Chelsea. Karma somehow arranged the whole thing to throw Bigfoot off of the real Chelsea's trail. Because if she knew that the real Chelsea Kettering was her intern, Chelsea—or should I say Chutney?—Jennings, it would be all over the front page of the* New York Post *tomorrow morning.*

"I've tried to call Chelsea in Australia three more times to see if I could get her to change her mind," Roxanne said, adjusting her foot on her desk. "All I ever get is an answering machine."

"She was pretty adamant about not wanting to have anything to do with *Trash*," Karma said innocently.

"I didn't get where I am by taking no for an answer," Bigfoot snapped.

Yeah, we know exactly how you got where you are, Lisha thought. *You sure didn't say no to sex with Barry Bassinger.*

"The three guests we have lined up are excellent," Chelsea said.

"Right," Karma agreed. "So we won't really miss Chelsea Kettering at all."

"We won't have to miss her," Roxanne said smugly.

The interns looked at her blankly.

"We won't have to, because I have a plan to get her to say yes."

Chelsea's face grew pale. "Wha-what would that be?"

Bigfoot leaned forward as far as her cast would allow. "Jazz wants us to offer ten thousand dollars to anyone who can convince Chelsea Kettering to come on *Trash.*"

"Bad idea, won't work," Karma said quickly.

"Right," Chelsea agreed. "Because . . . she can't be bought!"

"Clearly you don't get the *Trash* motto—it's all *Trash*. You see, everyone can be bought, it's just that some people have a higher price than others," Roxanne replied. "Here's the deal. We do this publicity blitz, with the story of what happened with her dad, and then photos of her then and now. We say we know she's in Australia, her address, and all that. And anyone who can convince her to come on *Trash* gets this money. And if it doesn't work, we up the sum."

Lisha snuck another peek at her watch. *One-fifteen. Fifteen minutes until I'm supposed to meet Harley,* she thought. Sweat began to break out on her forehead.

"But . . . but isn't that an invasion of her privacy, or something?" Chelsea asked nervously.

"Why would I care?" Roxanne asked.

"Because of legal implications," Karma said. "Yeah. I'm sure it's illegal. You could get sued."

"I doubt it," Roxanne said dismissively. "Jazz loves this idea. And freelance photographers are going to go nuts down in Australia, trying to catch this chick and get a current photo of her. It's kind of brilliant, if I do say so myself."

"I don't really see why you're so obsessed with this one particular girl," Chelsea said, trying to sound nonchalant.

"I'm not obsessed," Bigfoot corrected her. "But I always win, and I always get what I want." She turned to Lisha. "What do you think?"

"I think you're obsessed, too," Lisha said.

"Oh, really," Roxanne said sweetly. "Well, in case it escapes the combined and extremely limited wisdom of you three mental giants, you were not hired to *think.*"

"But you just asked me what I—" Lisha began.

"It was a trick question," Bigfoot replied. "You

were hired to follow orders and I have a whole bunch of them. Get ready to take scrupulous notes."

Roxanne went on and on, giving them a million assignments, everything from publicity for the Ten Thousand Dollars for Chelsea Kettering Campaign, to cleaning the employees' lounge.

Lisha furtively looked at her watch again. *It's one-thirty. But I can't just leave—I'll lose my job. And Bigfoot is on a roll. Who knows when she'll be done? But what if I don't show up to meet Harley? What will he do?*

". . . and another thing," Roxanne continued. "About walking Jazz's dogs. Sumtimes hasn't been hard enough on you. The dogs aren't getting enough exercise. I expect you to trot with them for at least three blocks. . . ."

One-forty. Will she ever stop talking?

". . . when you seat the audience for the shows, you need to look a lot better than you guys look today," Roxanne said. "I mean, Chelsea, what is that pathetic little outfit? You don't even look like someone we'd let into the studio, much less like someone who is hip enough to work here. . . ."

One forty-five. I can feel the sweat pouring off of me. I feel like I'm going to faint. Or throw up. Or—

"Lisha, are you okay?" Chelsea asked, breaking into Lisha's thoughts.

Lisha could feel Bigfoot, Karma, and Chelsea all staring at her.

Here's my chance, she thought.

"No, I . . . I think I'm sick," she said, rising quickly. "Excuse me—"

"You want me to come with—" Chelsea began.

"Sit!" Bigfoot barked. "She can go hurl by herself."

Lisha rushed out of the office, ran down the hall, and quickly took the stairs to the third floor. No one was around. She ducked into the film storage room, breathing hard.

At first the room seemed completely black. Then, as her eyes adjusted to the lack of light, she could make out shadows, bins of stored film stacked high.

"Harley?" she whispered.

No answer.

She wiped the sweat from her brow and took a few tentative steps toward the stacked film. "Harley?" she asked again.

Something crawled over her hand, and she screamed in fright.

A spider. She shook it off.

"Harley?" she called one more time.

But the only answer was the fearful pounding of her own heart.

He must have thought I stood him up, and he left, Lisha thought. *Which means he's mad. Really mad.*

I don't have any idea what he'll do next. But I know there's one thing I can be sure of.

He'll be back.

6

Lisha rounded the corner on her way to the studio where *Trash* was actually taped, lost in thought.

I know I should have called the lawyer last night, but I didn't, she thought guiltily. *I keep thinking that if I can just talk to Harley, I can reason with him. Which is crazy. But a lawyer is going to tell me to talk to the FBI before they come to talk to me, or something. For all I know they'll extradite me to France, and I'll end up in a French prison, and—*

Ooof.

Lisha bumped into something tall and hard. It was huge Demetrius, standing in the hallway outside the studio, his arms around tiny Karma.

"Sorry," Lisha said.

"No prob," Demetrius returned easily, his arms still wrapped around Karma. "You helping to seat the audience for today's show?"

"Yeah," Lisha said. "Are you doing the preshow?"

Either Demetrius or Roxanne always did the show before the on-air show, which always involved something wild, guaranteed to raise the audience's enthusiasm to a fever pitch.

"Roxanne's doing it," Demetrius said. "I'm on audience patrol, too."

"Me, too," Karma added, leaning her head against Demetrius's chest, which she barely reached, even in high heels.

"The two of you look disgustingly happy together," Lisha said.

"I know, we're nauseating," Karma agreed happily. "Hey, did you get the memo about the *Rave* interviews tomorrow?"

"No," Lisha said. "But my desk is a mess, so I could have missed it."

"Well, that Lydia Love is coming here tomorrow at three," Karma said. "We're all supposed to be available. I think the idea is that Sumtimes can exert more control over the interviews if they get done here at the Trash-bin."

Lisha shrugged. "I wasn't exactly planning to bare my soul to *Rave,* anyway."

"Have you called the lawyer about your boyfriend?" Demetrius asked.

"He's my *ex*-boyfriend," Lisha corrected. "And I'm—"

"Lisha!" Brian Bassinger called to her as he came barreling down the hallway, carrying a stack of Xeroxed papers. "Hi!"

"Hi, Brian," Lisha replied. "What is it?"

"Oh, nothing," Brian said. "I'm just in a good mood!"

"Oh, well, that's nice," Lisha said.

"Yeah, well, see ya." Brian stared at her dreamily, then he walked away.

"Strange guy," Karma commented.

"We were talking about Harley," Demetrius reminded them.

"As I was saying," Lisha said, "I'm on top of the situation."

Demetrius gave her a jaded look. "I take it that means you haven't called."

"Don't pressure me—"

"I'm sorry, Lisha, but I *am* going to pressure you," Demetrius said. "You need to—"

"I can't talk about this right now," Lisha interrupted, and she hurried into the *Trash* studio.

"Lish—" Karma called after her, but Lisha ignored her.

I know they're right, Lisha thought. *Okay. Right after the show, I'll go call the lawyer. I'll see if I can get information without giving him my name or anything. That's a good plan.*

"Hi," Chelsea said as Lisha joined her in the back of Studio A.

"What are you waiting for, an invitation to the prom?" Bigfoot hissed as she hobbled by them. "Get to work!"

Work meant that when Demetrius gave the signal, the rear doors would open, and the long line of young people waiting to be seated in the audience would stampede into the studio.

"Bigfoot is such a lovely person," Chelsea said.

"The loveliest," Lisha agreed. "Okay, I take it it's the usual—pretty people down front where the camera will pick them up, unattractive people in the back—"

"Sumtimes says she has to talk to us before we seat anyone today," Karma said, hurrying toward them.

Sumtimes finished a conversation with one of the cameramen then hurried over to the girls. A portable walkie-talkie headset was wrapped around her head, the mouthpiece near her mouth. "Okay, you guys, today don't seat any pretty people down front. Today's different. Gorgeous people go in the back row. Pleasant-looking people go in the middle. Unattractive people go in the front row. Got it?"

"How come?" Karma asked.

"Because that's how Jazz wants it," Sumtimes said patiently.

"But you always tell us to put the hip, good-looking people in the front—"

"Not today," Sumtimes said. She turned on her walkie-talkie. "D? You about ready?"

"Ready," came Demetrius's voice through the headset. "You want me to let 'em in?"

"It's a go," Sumtimes told him. "Let's open the pearly gates." She turned her head back to the interns. "Remember what I told you about the seating. And remember the *Trash* motto: You're too cool to care."

Chelsea made a face. "I hate being rude to people just because—"

"Don't think of it as rude," Sumtimes said. "Think of it as performance art."

As the rear doors opened, hordes of people streamed into the studio.

"You take the rear," Lisha told Karma, "you take the middle," she told Chelsea, "and I guess I'll take the front," she finished, hurrying down the aisle.

Two gorgeous girls in tiny miniskirts were heading for the front row.

"Sorry, these seats are reserved," Lisha told them.

"They are not," the blonder of the two girls stated. "And the front row gets on camera."

"I know, and you won't be sitting there," Lisha said coolly.

"We don't have to put up with that," the other girl said, outraged.

"True," Lisha said. "You could leave. I don't care."

The two girls made huffy sounds, but they turned and marched to the back of the studio. Meanwhile Karma and Chelsea were sending unattractive people down to Lisha.

"Great, just fill in these seats," Lisha told them, waving them down the aisle.

"This is way rad, Tracey," a skinny girl with braces and a bad perm told her friend as she settled into the front row.

"Way," her friend agreed. She had a huge nose, a

bad complexion, and massive thighs. "I never thought we'd score front-row seats!"

"Hi, I got sent to help," Nick said, strolling over to her. "What's the deal with the unattractive people down front today?"

"Ours is not to reason why," Lisha said. "We are but lowly interns, who live to serve." A couple came in with matching beer bellies, as well as matching denim jackets, and sauntered down the aisle.

"Yeah, here is cool," Nick told them.

"Wow!" the girl said, staring at Nick. "Did anyone ever tell you you look just like Brad Pitt?"

"He *is* Brad Pitt," Lisha said.

"He ain't really Brad Pitt," the boyfriend said as they found their seats. But the girlfriend kept looking back at Nick, as if she wasn't sure.

"This is so bogus," Nick told Lisha. "Separating people on the basis of their looks—pure *Trash*."

"Well, Jazz would say life is *Trash*," Lisha said. "I mean, people judge people on the basis of their looks all the time."

Like me, Lisha thought as she waved more people into the first few rows. *When I was fat and ugly, I had no life. If I hadn't been so insecure about my looks, I never would have fallen for Harley. Harley. How did he get past the* Trash *guards?*

What does he want from me?

"Okay, here we go," Karma said as she stood up in the *Trash* control room, looking down at the set.

Lisha, Chelsea, and Nick were there, too, having

been given permission for the first time to watch the show from the booth. Sky was in there, too, but he was sitting with a set of acoustic headphones on, in front of one of the soundboard panels. Down below them, Roxanne was just finishing her warm-up with the audience, something having to do with finding money hidden inside the clothing of people who were total strangers to each other.

"It's great watching from in here," Nick said.

"Hey, Nick, mon, Jazz is wanting you," Winston Manroot, Jazz's secretary, said in his lilting accent as he stuck his head in the door.

"For what?" Nick asked, scowling.

"If you think she tells me, you are on some serious drugs, mon," Winston said. He shook his head and his dreadlocks went flying. "She says jump—you know the drill."

"Unfortunately," Nick said.

Winston flashed his fabulous grin. "It could be worse, mon," he said cheerfully. "Bigfoot could be callin' on you."

Lisha's jaw dropped open. "How did you know we call her—" She stopped herself. The director and his assistant could hear every word they said.

Winston winked at Lisha. "No secrets around here, mon," he said, and disappeared out the door.

"I'll catch you guys later," Nick said, and left.

Chelsea's jaw set hard.

"Don't get weird about Jazz and Nick," Karma told her. "It's probably nothing."

"Yeah, but what if it's—"

91

"Okay, guys, cut the talking," Sky said. "We're on in ten."

"Count it down," the director said, focusing in on the main monitor.

"Ten, nine, eight . . ." Sky began.

"We're live," the director said into his headset, when Sky finished the countdown. "Camera one, stage right to Jazz."

As a rule, Jazz made a creative entrance. The audience—both in the studio and at home—never knew what to expect. Roxanne had driven the audience into a frenzy, and now they all stood up, chanting "Jazz! Jazz! Jazz!"

Today, two cute guys dressed in medical scrubs entered from stage right, wheeling a hospital gurney, on which there lay a body.

The gurney was upended, and the body practically flew off into the air, and then landed deftly on its feet.

It was Jazz, her body completely swathed in bandages, like a mummy. Only her face, and her perfect, long white-blond hair were free.

"She's trussed up like a mummy?" Karma asked, bewildered.

"Now, this is out there, even for Jazz," Lisha said.

"Shhh!" Sky instructed them.

The audience had no idea what Jazz was up to, but they went wild, anyway, as the "applause" signs flashed on and off.

Jazz held up one finger to quiet them, and they

obeyed, sat, and leaned forward to hear what Jazz's latest stunt would be.

"Well, well, well," Jazz said, standing in the middle of the *Trash* set, surveying the audience, "what have we here? In the front two rows?"

Lisha looked, through the control-room glass, at the people in the front rows. They were looking at each other uncomfortably, wondering what Jazz had in store for them.

"So, you guys have read all the tabloid crap they write about me, I'm sure," Jazz said conversationally. "Last week I read that I had sex with the entire cast of *Mad About You,* including the dog!"

The audience laughed and applauded.

"How utterly *Trash*y," Jazz continued. "This same article said I have had plastic surgery on every part of my face and body. Well, that's not true."

"Close-up on camera two," the director called into his headset. A camera moved in on a close-up of Jazz's face.

"For example, I was born with this forehead," Jazz said with a wicked smile. At that moment two incredibly fine guys came out from the wings, and cut Jazz out of her bandages, as the audience roared their approval. Underneath she was wearing a simple white bikini.

"I was not, however," Jazz said, "born with this body." Her eyes scanned the people sitting in the front rows.

"Who put these people here?" she demanded.

No answer.

"You people in the first two rows, stand up!" Jazz commanded.

They all stood up.

She walked up to one of the people in the front row—Lisha saw it was one of the first two girls she had seated.

"Hi," Jazz said, draping her arm around the girl.

"Hi," the girl squeaked, staring up, awestruck, at Jazz. "It's really you!"

Everyone laughed.

"What's your name?" Jazz asked conversationally.

"Tracey Angier," the girl said.

"Tracey," Jazz said, "I wasn't born gorgeous, you know."

"Really?" Tracey asked, wide-eyed.

"Anyone can look good," Jazz said. "Have you ever thought about plastic surgery?"

"Well, yeah," Tracey said. "I guess. I mean, it's really expensive and stuff—"

"What if it wasn't expensive?" Jazz asked her. "What would you have done?"

"You need everything done, baby!" some guy yelled from the back of the house.

Some of the audience laughed. Tracey blushed.

"Too bad we can't do plastic surgery on his mind, isn't it?" Jazz said coolly.

Tracey hugged Jazz. "You're my idol."

"Thanks," Jazz said. "Now, back to the subject at hand. If cost was no object, what would you have done?"

"A nose job," Tracey said. "Something on my

94

skin to get rid of the marks—I used to have all this gross acne. And, um, that liposuction stuff on my thighs."

"Cool," Jazz said. "And how many others in these front two rows have thought about plastic surgery?"

Most of the people raised their hands.

That's why she wanted not-so-good-looking people down in front, Lisha realized. *But where is she going with this whole thing?*

The answer came soon enough.

"Fantastic!" Jazz said, taking Tracey's arm, and then pointing with her handheld mike at two other girls and three guys in the front rows. "You, you, you, you, and you," she ordered. "Up on the set. In the director chairs. And Tracey here, too."

Lisha watched, amazed.

When the six teens were all seated, Jazz sat down on the famous *Trash* couch, with her arm around the male half of the ever-present plastic blowup doll couple that graced the set of *Trash*. Today both dolls were also swathed in white bandages.

Jazz reached for a handful of M&M's from the jar she kept on the coffee table. "So, who's under the age of eighteen?" She threw a handful of candy into her mouth.

Nobody said anything.

"Cool," Jazz said. "And if you're lying, we'll find out, and you're outta this. Okay, we're going to play a little game now. I call it the Obnoxious Game. I'm going to ask you guys a question, and

we'll see who can come up with the most obnoxious answer."

"What do we win?" a guy with no chin and less
hair asked from his place in the center chair on
stage.

"Not telling," Jazz said coolly. "But it's something fantastic, I promise. Wanna play, anyway?"

They all nodded yes. "Okay," Jazz said, "here
goes. What's the most obnoxious thing that you can
say to someone at a funeral, about the dearly de-
parted?"

"Uh . . . this girl I know got treated by the same
doctor. She's dead now, too," the girl on the end offered.

"Oooooo," the audience reacted.

"You know, he owed me ten bucks!" the balding
guy shouted out.

The audience laughed.

"I wish she could know that she looks a lot better now with short hair!" Tracey called out.

This time the oohs and ahhs and whistles were
loud enough to be heard in the control room.

"He's allergic to dirt, you know," another guy
cried.

The audience cracked up.

"Damn, I can't believe I'm missing *Ricki Lake*
for this!" the last guy said.

The audience cracked up even louder.

"You would have thought there'd be more people
here, huh?" the last girl said.

This time even the people in the control room
had to laugh.

"Okay, it's sick," Karma said, "but it is funny."

Lisha nodded, her eyes glued to the stage below.

Jazz turned and faced one of the cameras, which came in tight as the director issued orders into his headset. Lisha shifted her gaze to the monitors in the control room, all of which showed Jazz in extreme close-up.

"Beauty is skin-deep, right, gang?" Jazz asked. "And it's what's inside that counts, isn't that what adults love to tell you? We'll see. Because on today's *Trash,* we're going to have a contest to pick which of these six plastic-surgery candidates is the most obnoxious of them all. And then *Trash* is going to give that person, all expenses paid, all the plastic surgery they ever wanted! And then we'll see how it changes their life! Or not! Back in a moment with more *Trash.*"

The audience whooped and hollered and cheered and stood and applauded as the studio lights went out for a commercial break.

"Genius," Karma repeated. "Demented, sick, disturbed, perverted, and thoroughly ill. But genius, all the same."

Lisha was lost in thought as she got off the elevator on her floor. Right before she'd left the office, she had tried the number of the criminal lawyer that Karma had given her. He had not been available, but Lisha left a message for him to return her call.

At least I did something, Lisha thought, secretly glad that the lawyer hadn't been available. *At least it's a step.*

"Hi," Sky said as Lisha rounded the corner to the hall of her apartment. Sky had his key in the lock of his own apartment, about to enter.

"Hi," Lisha responded. "Just get home?"

"I went out for sushi with Alan."

"Raw fish?" Lisha said, making a face.

"Yeah, I agree. Alan could live on it. I pushed it around on my plate hoping it wasn't going to flop on its own. Did you eat?"

"I stayed late at the office to finish some filing Bigfoot wanted done."

"We could go and get a burger on the corner," Sky offered.

"No, thanks," Lisha said. "I'm beat."

"Or maybe you're just avoiding me," Sky said.

"I'm not, I'm just tired," Lisha insisted.

Sky scratched his chin. "Would you say yes if Alan asked you?"

"This isn't about you or Alan, okay?" Lisha said.

Sky came over to her and looked into her eyes. "Are you and Alan in a thing with each other?"

"I don't even know what that means," Lisha said crossly.

"Yeah, you do," Sky said. "Alan is my friend. But you don't belong with him."

Lisha gazed back up at Sky. She tried to keep her voice cool—much cooler than she really felt, every time he was near her. *You'll hurt me, Sky,* she wanted to blurt out. *And I'll hurt you. I know it.*

"Look, Sky, you don't know me at all, really—"

"That's not true—"

"There's just . . . it's complicated," Lisha said, her voice low.

"I can handle complicated," Sky said.

"Not this complicated," Lisha replied.

"Give me a chance—"

"I don't want to get involved—"

"With me?" Sky interrupted. "Or at all?"

"Just . . . you just have to back off," Lisha said. She took a step away from him. "Just . . . back off."

"You don't really want Alan," Sky said earnestly. "I just don't believe—" He stopped himself. Then he took Lisha in his arms, and kissed her passionately.

For a moment she was lost in the best, hottest kiss she had ever had in her life.

But then she pulled herself away from him. "You jerk!" she yelled.

"Yeah, I'm a jerk!" Sky said, his eyes blazing. "So tell me you didn't really want me to kiss you, that you didn't feel that, and I'll leave you alone—"

"I don't have to tell you anything," Lisha said furiously as she quickly began to unlock the many locks on the door to her apartment.

"Lisha—"

"Leave me alone," she said as she slammed into her apartment, leaving Sky in the hallway, still staring after her.

"Sky," she whispered to herself, leaning her back against the door to the apartment. "Sky."

The apartment was dark and deserted. Karma had plans with Demetrius before her shift at Jimi's. Chelsea was with Nick.

Peace, that's what I want, Lisha thought. *Everything is so peaceful with Alan. I don't want to feel a passion that sweeps me away. I don't. I just want to get rid of Harley, and not think about Sky, and simplify my life.*

She pushed out of her sandals and padded over to the answering machine.

The on-light was blinking.

Lisha shuddered. She had a very bad feeling. She pressed the button.

It wasn't Harley. It was Lydia Love, asking for an off-the-record interview for *Rave.*

"Yeah, I'll bet it's off-the-record," Lisha muttered.

The phone rang. Lisha picked it up.

"Yeah," she answered.

"Lisha," a voice whispered to her.

Male. Low. Disguised.

Lisha froze. Unable to say anything, unable to put the phone down.

"Listen, Lisha," the eerie, whispered voice repeated. "You missed our meeting. That wasn't smart. But I'm a nice guy and I'm offering a second chance. Your last chance. Tomorrow, eight-thirty in the morning. Same place. You—"

Lisha slammed the phone down.

"Damn you, Harley!" she cried as tears ran down her face. "I'm not running scared anymore! Do you hear me? I'm going to find a way to get rid of you. Once and for all!"

Sometime after midnight, Chelsea unlocked the front door of the dark apartment and tiptoed in so that she wouldn't wake up her roommates.

"Hi," Lisha said, from where she sat on the couch.

Chelsea yelped and jumped into the air. "Lish? You scared me to death! What are you doing sitting in the dark?"

"Contemplating the sewer that is currently called my life," Lisha said.

"What happened?" Chelsea asked, coming over to sit next to her on the couch. "Oh, God, was Harley here?"

"Who knows?" Lisha shrugged. "Sometimes he leaves calling cards, and sometimes he doesn't."

"What are you talking about? Can I turn the light on?"

"No, I like the dark." Lisha sighed and threw her head back on the couch. "I have made such a mess of everything, Chelsea. I wish life was just some big game, and when you mess up you get to call 'do over.'"

"What's wrong?" Chelsea asked anxiously. "You're not pregnant, are you?"

Lisha laughed a bitter laugh. "Hardly. I live like a vestal virgin these days."

"I thought maybe you and Sky finally admitted that you're crazy for each other and then something went wrong," Chelsea admitted.

"I told you, there's nothing going on between me and Sky," Lisha said firmly.

"You and Alan, then—"

"My problem is not a current-guy problem, it's a past-guy problem," Lisha said. "Namely—you guessed it—Harley." She turned toward Chelsea. She could barely make out her friend's features in the darkened living room. "Here's what happened."

Lisha told Chelsea about the note on her desk, about how she had gotten to the meeting late, and how Harley had called and threatened her if she didn't meet him at the same place tomorrow morning at eight-thirty.

"He sounded so creepy on the phone," Lisha recalled with a shudder. "He whispered, like something out of one of those bad psycho murder movies."

"Wait, you're telling me that after you got that note from him, you went to meet him alone yesterday?" Chelsea asked incredulously. "Are you out of your mind?"

"Probably," Lisha replied. "What was I supposed to do, bring the welcome wagon?"

"You have to go to the police!" Chelsea exclaimed.

"And get extradited to France? And thrown in prison for transporting drugs?" Lisha asked, her voice rising hysterically. "Are you out of your mind?"

Chelsea was silent for a moment. She reached for Lisha's hand in the dark. "Let's try to look at this logically. Do you have the note he left where he threatened you? In case the police need it?"

"I have it," Lisha said. "But he didn't sign his name."

"Then how do you know Harley left the note?" Chelsea asked. "It could have been anybody!"

"I'm so sure," Lisha snorted. "I don't know any other psychotics who are stalking me."

"But how could Harley have gotten into the *Trash* offices?" Chelsea asked. "There are guards downstairs, and they check ID, and Harley doesn't have clearance—"

"I don't know how, but he managed," Lisha said. "I wish I could just—"

They heard their front door being unlocked, and both girls froze. Then, as if by unspoken agreement, they both jumped up and ran into the kitchen, ducking behind the counter. Chelsea grabbed the portable phone, ready to dial 911.

Someone came into the apartment. Slowly, Lisha

103

raised her head so that her eyes peeked over the top of the counter. "It's Karma," she said with relief. She and Chelsea both stood up.

Karma whirled around. "Have you two lost it?" she asked. "What are you doing in the dark on the kitchen floor?"

"It's the best way to find the cockroaches," Lisha joked, her voice flat.

"We were afraid you were Harley," Chelsea said, turning on the kitchen light. She looked at her watch. "It's too early for you to be here."

"It was a slow night at Jimi's, so Arnold let me leave early," Karma explained. "What's going on?"

"You tell her," Lisha told Chelsea. "I can't go through the whole thing again."

Chelsea brought Karma up to date. "Did I leave anything out?" she asked Lisha, when she'd finished.

"Only that I called the lawyer today," Lisha said. "I didn't get a chance to tell you that. He wasn't available—some flunky told me he'd return my call."

"So, you're saying that the note wasn't signed, and that Harley whispered over the phone?" Karma asked, massaging her tired feet. "What if it wasn't Harley?"

"I asked her the same thing," Chelsea pointed out.

"Wishful thinking," Lisha said.

"Not necessarily," Karma pointed out. "It really is hard to get past those guards downstairs at *Trash,* you know. What if it's . . . Brian!"

"Brian *Bassinger*?" Lisha asked incredulously. "Brian Weenie *Bassinger*?"

"Well, you have to admit, he seems to have this huge crush on you," Chelsea said.

"And he'd have access to every place at *Trash*," Karma pointed out. "He'd know about the film storage room. How would Harley?"

"He's psychotic, not stupid," Lisha said. "He followed me. He skulked around or something—"

"Sounds dubious," Karma decided.

"Who cares if it's dubious?" Lisha asked. "I'm just telling you, it's Harley! And if I don't meet him tomorrow morning, my butt is fried!"

"But if you do meet him, he could do something terrible to you!" Chelsea cried. "He has a gun, remember?"

"So what am I supposed to do, then?" Lisha asked. "And don't tell me to go to the police, because—"

"I have an idea," Karma interrupted. "You go meet this mystery guy—"

"Karma, it isn't safe—" Chelsea began.

"Hold your horses, I'm not through," Karma said, chewing on a piece of her hair contemplatively. "Lisha meets the guy, but we go with her. We call Demetrius tonight and bring him in on this. Then tomorrow we have Demetrius stand guard for us outside the door, but the mystery guy inside won't know Demetrius is outside. That way if it's Harley, and he has a gun, Demetrius can go for help before anything can happen."

"Are you on drugs?" Lisha asked. "I'm not letting all of you risk your lives because my ex is crazy!"

"It's either that, or we call the cops tonight," Karma said. "Because no way are we letting you go to this meeting alone."

"It's a stupid plan," Lisha said. "But okay."

"I feel like throwing up," Lisha said, her hands on her stomach.

"Hang in there." Demetrius patted her back.

It was the following morning, about eight-fifteen, and Lisha, Chelsea, Karma, and Demetrius were all in the lobby of the *Trash* building.

"I'm kind of nervous, too," Chelsea admitted.

"Look, this is crazy," Lisha said. "I'll go by myself—"

"Forget it," Karma said. "This is going to work."

"But this is it, Lisha," Demetrius said sternly. "You speak to the attorney today or we're going to call and speak to him for you."

"I will, I promise," Lisha told him. "I can't live my life like this anymore."

"Okay," Karma said. "One for all and all for one, right?" She put her arm straight out, and one by one they each laid their hands on top of hers.

"Let's go do it," Demetrius said.

The guard knew them, and he nodded as they passed. Silently, they took the elevator up to the third floor.

"Now remember," Demetrius said, "you have to talk loud enough in there so that I can hear you outside in the hallway. There's no other way out of that room except by me."

Lisha nodded, and the three girls walked down to the door of the film storage room and opened it.

Lisha went in first.

It was pitch-black, even darker, it seemed, than the afternoon before. Lisha could feel Karma and Chelsea right behind her.

"Harley?" Lisha whispered. "I'm here, just like you told me."

No answer.

Now Lisha could make out the tall piles of film canisters that surrounded her. But she couldn't see Harley.

"Harley?" she called again. "We have to talk. I . . . I want to help you. . . ."

They heard the sounds of something rustling between two of the stacks of film. Lisha jumped, and grabbed Karma with one hand and Chelsea with the other.

"I'm going to turn on the light," Lisha said, reaching toward the light switch on the wall.

"No!" a male voice whispered frantically from behind a tall stack of film.

Lisha's grip tightened on her friends' hands.

She gulped hard. "Wha-what do you want?"

"You," the voice whispered.

"Harley, is that you?" Lisha asked.

No answer.

"I'm not alone, Harley," she said, trying to sound confident. "My friends are here, too."

"What friends?" the voice whispered.

"The ones you met at my apartment the other night," Lisha said, her voice loud enough to carry to Demetrius in the hall.

"Who's Harley?" the voice said.

Lisha's jaw dropped open. "Are you playing mind games with me, Harley?"

No answer.

"Brian?" Karma called tentatively. "Is that you?"

"Brian Bassinger?" Chelsea called.

"Forget it," the male voice whispered. "Just go away and forget it."

"It *is* Brian," Chelsea said. "I'm turning on the light."

"No—!"

It was too late. The light was flipped on. The girls peered behind the stack of film.

Crouched down, looking up at them, was Jazz's gorgeous Jamaican secretary, Winston Manroot.

"Winston?" Lisha cried in disbelief. "Are you out of your mind?"

Winston stood up and brushed some dust out of his dreadlocks. "Surprise," he said weakly.

"What is all this?" Chelsea asked. "Are you crazy?"

"Well, now that you mention it, I do feel like somethin' of an idiot," Winston admitted. "This was just supposed to be a goof, mon. Who is Harley?"

"A *goof?*" Lisha echoed. "That note and that phone call, a *goof?*"

"And what were you threatening Lisha about, anyway?" Chelsea added.

"The film," Winston said. "The hidden camera in

Jazz's office. What did you think I was referrin' to, girl?"

The girls' jaws dropped open.

"Well, you interns planted that hidden camera, didn't you?" Winston asked, brushing one of his dreadlocks out of his face.

"Wait, I'd better go call off Demetrius," Karma said. "He'll come running in here with the guards in about thirty seconds. Don't say a word till I get back, because I have to hear all of this."

Karma went out to Demetrius, quickly explained that they weren't in any danger, then returned into the storage room. "Okay, spill it," she demanded.

"Well, I feel like quite the fool now," Winston said. "See, I found your camera—it *was* your camera, right?"

"Maybe," Lisha hedged.

"Yeah-mon, it's yours," Winston said. "I saw one of your buds, Sky, goin' into Jazz's office one morning, carryin' something small. He didn't see me. When I was sortin' through Jazz's bookcase, I found the camera, and then I put two and two together. I took the film home."

"So you were threatening Lisha about the hidden camera?" Karma asked. "Why didn't you threaten Sky?"

"Sky doesn't have anything I want," Winston said, flashing his killer smile. "My guess was that all of you interns are in on something together, something with that camera. Am I right?"

The girls traded looks. "What is it that you want?" Lisha asked.

"Well, now I'm feelin' kind of like the hind side of a donkey," Winston singsonged. "This was supposed to be a cute way to get to know you."

"You're kidding," Lisha said flatly.

"No," Winston said. "I'm not."

"Didn't you ever hear of asking a girl out for coffee?" Karma asked, exasperated.

"I was trying to be creative," Winston admitted. "By the way, who is Harley?"

"Never mind," Lisha said quickly. "What are you planning to do with the film you found?"

"Nothing," Winston said with a shrug.

"Nothing?" Karma repeated.

"What, you thought I was goin' to turn you in to the teen-queen she-devil, Jazz?" Winston asked. "Not on your life."

"But . . . but why?" Chelsea asked him.

"Just because I work for her doesn't mean I like her," Winston said. "What are you plannin' to do with that film, anyway?"

"Never mind," Lisha said quickly.

"Hey, is that any way to treat a nice guy who is going to keep your secret?" Winston asked.

"He's right," Chelsea said. "He could have busted us, and he didn't."

"He could still bust us," Lisha pointed out.

"Yeah, and we can bust him for his anonymous threatening notes and phone calls to a fellow employee," Karma pointed out.

"Okay, we're even," Winston said. "You'll tell me sometime, though, won't you?"

"Maybe," Lisha said.

"How about if I ask you out for coffee," Winston said, with a grin. "Will you tell me then?"

"Look, Winston, no offense, but I am just not looking for a relationship right now," Lisha said. "Besides, this whole thing has me really wigged out. That stupid note, and the phone call . . . say—how did you manage to disguise your voice and hide your Jamaican accent, anyway?"

"Oh, it's not difficult," Winston said, and there wasn't a trace of his singsong accent as he spoke. "I'm actually an actor. I have an audition for *Days of Our Lives* next week." He reached for Lisha's hand. "I'm really sorry if I scared you."

"You did," Lisha said, taking her hand back.

"Does this mean no coffee date?" Winston asked.

"What are you planning to do with our film?" Lisha asked.

Winston went back behind the film stack, reached for something, and handed it to Lisha. "Your film. I'm an honorable guy."

"Thank you," Lisha said.

"Now, about the coffee date—"

"How about if I think about it," Lisha said. "I have some important business to take care of before I think about anything else." She nodded at Chelsea and Karma. "I have to call a certain lawyer, and straighten out my life."

Lisha outlined her problem to the criminal lawyer, whose name was Sandy Dweck, in the broadest possible terms—that she might have done something illegal, even though she hadn't known she was doing it, that now someone was blackmailing her and stalking her about it. As she spoke she doodled nervously on the notepad on top of her desk. Then she looked around her tiny cubicle, worried that she'd be overheard, anxious about what Dweck would tell her.

Dweck had refused to talk to her unless she told him her name. And gave him an address where he could send his bill. Lisha did both.

Because I just can't live like this anymore, she realized. *Anything would be better than this.*

"Well, Miss Bishop, I will really need to hear your story in detail, in my office, so that I can take notes. And then I can give you some advice. When would be convenient for you?"

"How about tonight?" Lisha said quickly.

"I'm sorry," Mr. Dweck said, "I don't have evening office hours. And I'm booked up for the next couple of weeks. If you speak to my secretary—"

"No, you don't understand," Lisha said, gripping the phone. "The person who is stalking me—he broke into my apartment. He has a gun. He's dangerous. I . . . I have to do something right away!"

"You could go to the police—"

"No, I can't!" Lisha exclaimed. "Please! Couldn't you just help me? I'll only take a few minutes of your time, and then if you tell me I have to go to the police, I'll do it."

Mr. Dweck sighed into the phone. "If you could get over here right away, I could give you some time—"

"I will!" Lisha cried. "I'll get a taxi and I'll be right over. What's the address?"

Lisha quickly scribbled the lawyer's address in the notebook, thanked him again, and hung up. Then she grabbed her purse and hurried down to Sumtimes's office.

"Sumtimes?" Lisha said, trying to make her voice sound weak and pathetic.

Sumtimes looked up from the memo she was reading.

"I'm really feeling sick," Lisha said. "I think I need to go home."

"What are your symptoms?" Sumtimes asked.

"Headache, stomachache, chills—I think I have a fever."

"Okay, go home and go to bed," Sumtimes said. "Chicken soup works miracles."

"Thanks," Lisha said.

She dashed to the elevator, but couldn't stand the wait, and finally ran down the stairs to the lobby, where she almost collided with Winston, carrying some take-out food in a cardboard container.

"Hey, watch yourself, girl," he said, feinting to avoid her.

"Sorry," she said, hurrying past him.

"Wait up a second," Winston said.

Lisha sighed impatiently, but she stopped and turned to him. *He knows all about the Trash-cam,* she thought. *I don't want to tick him off or he could change his mind about turning us in to Jazz.*

"I'm sorry about this morning," Winston said sheepishly. "I'd like to do something to make it up to you."

"Just forget about it," Lisha said. "I have."

113

"Well, good." Winston smiled. "Then we can start all over again and I can impress you with my charming Jamaican ways."

"Look, I'm in a hurry, I've got an appointment," Lisha said. "We'll talk . . . later, okay?"

"Yeah-mon," Winston said. "I'll look forward to it."

Lisha hurried out to the street. "Taxi, taxi, where is a taxi when you need one?" she muttered, scanning the traffic down the block.

And then she realized something. She had forgotten to bring Mr. Dweck's address that she had scribbled in her notebook. *I can't go back up there and get it,* she realized. *What was it? Think, Lisha. Fifteen-forty Broadway. That's it!*

Lisha walked down the street and then turned uptown, desperately searching for a taxi. *That stupid cliché is true,* she thought. *There is never a taxi in this city when you need one.*

"Come on," she pleaded under her breath, "just one lousy empty cab is all I need—"

A hand reached out and grabbed her arm, pulling her in between two parked cars, and then across the sidewalk and into a building's entryway.

Lisha screamed, but another hand clamped over her mouth, muffling the sound.

Harley.

His eyes glittered at her. His grip was like a steel vise on her arm.

"Hi there, Lish," he said, smiling crazily. "I told you I'd be back."

"Now, if I take my hand off of your mouth, you have to be a good girl, and promise not to scream," Harley said, his voice low.

Lisha was so scared her entire body was vibrating. She managed to nod her head yes.

"Good," Harley said. "And just in case you try to pull anything, feel this." Lisha felt something hard poking into her back. "I would hate to use it on you, Lish. I really would."

She nodded again, her eyes two huge pools of fear.

Slowly, he took his hand away from her mouth. The sharp object—a knife, a gun?—was still poking into her back.

"This is amazing, Lisha, really. I didn't think I'd get to see you until you went out to lunch. But maybe your mind kinda heard my mind calling to you, or something. What do you think?"

"I don't know," she managed to say.

"Did you miss me?"

What should I say? What should I do? Lisha thought desperately. She forced her voice to sound steady.

"Harley, if you really care about me as much as you say you do, why do you keep pulling a gun on me?"

"Because I know how fickle girls can be," he said. "Especially you. You left me once. In London. Remember? You said you didn't want to have anything to do with me. That wasn't very nice, Lisha. I mean, I was the only guy who would even look twice at you when you were fat, remember?"

"You got me hooked on diet pills," Lisha reminded him angrily.

"Hey, baby, I didn't get you hooked. You got yourself hooked," Harley said.

A couple walked by on the street, arm in arm, laughing. Harley pulled Lisha farther into the entryway.

Please, look this way! Lisha thought. But the couple walked right by without ever glancing her way.

"What do you want?" Lisha asked desperately.

"First of all, I want a little respect!" Harley said, his voice rising dangerously. "You are going to talk to me with respect, got it?" He pushed the sharp object into her spine for emphasis.

"I got it," Lisha replied.

"That's better," Harley said. "Now, I have my

116

buddy's car parked a block from here. You and I are going for a ride."

"To where?" she asked fearfully.

"Someplace where we can be alone," he said.

"I was on my way to an appointment," Lisha said thinking frantically. "The person is expecting me, and then they're expecting me back at work. Everyone will be really suspicious if I don't show up. And my friends already know you broke into our apartment. They'll go to the police."

"Nice story, Lish," Harley said. "First of all, it takes twenty-four hours before the cops will bother to look for you. By that time you and I will be long gone."

"To where?" she asked again.

He didn't answer. Instead, he took his free hand and ran it from her cheek, down her throat, and over her right breast.

Lisha shuddered in revulsion.

"You used to love that," Harley said, his voice low. "Remember?"

Lisha tried to smile at Harley, but all she could manage was a slight grimace.

"Just walk in front of me, Lisha," he ordered. "If you do anything dumb, I *will* hurt you, baby. I mean, it would bum me out, but I'd do it. Okay, let's go."

Harley prodded her in her back, and she walked out of the doorway. Various people walked on the street, but they ignored her. No one seemed to find it odd that a white-faced young woman was walking down the street with a guy walking six inches behind her.

Please, God, Lisha prayed as she forced herself to put one foot in front of the other, *please let me figure out how to get out of this.*

Please. Let me get out of this alive.

"Lish?" Chelsea said, sticking her head in Lisha's cubicle late that morning.

The cubicle was empty. Chelsea had been so busy all morning that she hadn't had time to breathe. She hadn't even seen Lisha at all.

Sumtimes was walking by the area, recording a memo for herself into her tiny tape recorder. "If you're looking for Lisha, she went home sick a couple of hours ago," she said.

"She did?" Chelsea asked with surprise.

"Yeah, she said she thought she had the flu."

"Thanks for telling me." Chelsea went into Lisha's cubicle and sat behind her desk. Then she picked up the phone and called their apartment. The answering machine picked up. "Lisha, if you're there, pick up," she said into the phone. "I want to make sure you're okay."

"Hi, Chels," Alan said, stopping by the desk. "You heading up to Sicko Central? Because I am, and as you know, misery loves company."

"Yeah," Chelsea said, her voice troubled. "I stopped to get Lisha. She went home sick."

"No kidding?" Alan hesitated before continuing. "She's been really upset about something lately, hasn't she?"

118

"Yeah," Chelsea admitted, "she has."

"She wouldn't tell me what it was," Alan said. "You know how Lish is—Miss Mysterious."

"I know," Chelsea agreed, still staring at the phone.

"Do you know what's bothering her?" Alan asked.

Chelsea nodded yes.

Alan leaned against the wall of the tiny office. "And I have a feeling you're not going to tell me what it is."

"I can't," she said unhappily. "Lisha would have to tell you herself."

"So, did you call home to see how she's feeling?"

"I just did," Chelsea said. "The machine picked up."

"Maybe she's sleeping," Alan suggested.

"Maybe," she echoed, but her tone was doubtful. She looked down at Lisha's desk, and there, on the top of her notepad, was the name Mr. Dweck, and a Broadway address. Then, written in large letters and circled many times, were the words SEE ME NOW!!!

"Hello beloved *Trash*ophiles," Karma said in her nasal whine, coming up beside Alan. "I hear Sicko Central calling us. Where's Lish?"

Chelsea filled her in.

"But she didn't pick up the phone when I called home just now," Chelsea said anxiously. She lifted the notepad to Karma. "Do you know who Mr. Dweck is?"

"That's the lawyer I told her to call!" Karma said,

119

taking the pad. "See me now," she read out loud. "You think that's where she went?"

"I think we should call him," Chelsea decided.

"Okay, now you're scaring me," Alan said. "Why does Lisha need to see a criminal lawyer?"

Chelsea and Karma exchanged looks.

"We can't tell you," Karma said reluctantly.

"Come on," Alan cajoled. "I care about Lisha. A lot."

"We know you do," Chelsea said.

"But we can't tell you," Karma added. "Call the lawyer, Chels."

Chelsea quickly called information and got the phone number for Dweck, Levine and Powell, Mr. Dweck's law firm, and dialed the number.

"Mr. Dweck, please," Chelsea said when a female voice answered the phone.

"Who is calling?" the woman asked.

"Chelsea Jennings—"

"No, no," Karma said, grabbing the phone from her. "Hello? Tell Mr. Dweck that Primrose Jensen is on the phone. Yes, I'll hold."

"Who is Primrose Jensen?" Chelsea asked.

"My broker," Karma said. "She's a friend of his. This way he'll take the call."

"Rose?" a male voice said into the phone.

"I'm sorry, Mr. Dweck, but this is actually a client of Ms. Jensen's," Karma said quickly. "I just needed to make sure you would actually get on the phone."

"Look, Miss—" Mr. Dweck began.

"I'm sorry I misrepresented myself," Karma continued, "but this is really important. Like life-and-death-type important. I'm a friend of Lisha Bishop's. I think maybe you had an appointment with her, and I'm concerned with whether or not she ever made it to the meeting."

"I'm sorry, Miss—whoever you are—but I don't give out information as to whom I meet with or who my clients are. It's privileged information. Now, if you'll excuse me—"

"No, you don't understand," Karma said. "I'm the person who recommended you to Lisha, through Primrose. You can call Primrose and check me out, if you don't believe me. The name is Karma Kushner. And I know all about attorney-client privilege. But see, Lisha was coming to see you because her ex-boyfriend was stalking her. And now we think she might be missing. So, that's why I need to know if she had an appointment with you, and if she showed up. I really need your help."

Mr. Dweck sighed into the phone. "All right. I did receive a call from Miss Bishop," he admitted. "She mentioned something about . . . well, she mentioned that she might be in some trouble. I told her that if she came over right away, I would try to offer some advice. She told me she'd be right over."

"What time did you speak with her?" Karma asked.

"Early this morning," Mr. Luger said. "And in answer to your next question, no, she did not show up."

"Thank you for your help," Karma said, and

121

hung up. She quickly told Chelsea and Alan what the lawyer had told her.

"I'm getting a really terrible feeling about this," Chelsea said.

"About what?" Alan asked in frustration. "What am I supposed to do, just assume the worst? You guys have to tell me what's going on!"

Chelsea and Karma looked at each other again.

"Should we tell him?" Chelsea asked.

"Let's try our number again first," Karma said. She dialed their home phone quickly. And got the machine again. "Lisha, if you can hear me, or if you get my message, call us at work right away. We are really worried about you!"

She hung up.

"Okay, that's it," Alan declared. "We're not leaving until you tell me what's going on."

"I think we should," Chelsea decided.

Karma nodded in agreement.

Quickly Chelsea filled Alan in on the whole story. Alan grew more and more shocked as the story progressed.

"Wow, I couldn't have invented this plot if I tried to," Alan said, shaking his head, when Chelsea had concluded Lisha's story. "We've got to go to the police."

"That's exactly what Lisha didn't want us to do," Karma pointed out. "Her whole life could be wrecked."

"Yeah, well, she could also get killed by this Harley nut, which somehow seems worse, don't you think?" Alan said sharply.

"One of us should go back to the apartment to see if she's there," Chelsea suggested. "I'll make some excuse and go—"

"What is going on in here?" Roxanne demanded, storming into the cubicle and throwing a stack of files on Lisha's desk. "Where's Bishop?"

"She went home sick," Alan replied.

"Interns don't get sick," Roxanne said. "And what does that have to do with the three of you in here wasting time?" she asked suspiciously, balancing herself on her good foot.

"We were just on our way to Sicko—I mean, to work in the transcribing room," Karma told Roxanne.

"So, go!" Roxanne ordered.

"I, uh, think I'm not feeling very well, either," Chelsea improvised. "Would you mind very much if I went home—"

"Yes, I'd mind," Bigfoot snapped. "If I can put in more than a full day with my foot killing me, you can finish out your day with a little sniffle."

"It's more than a sniffle," Chelsea lied. "It's . . . my stomach. Food poisoning, maybe." She held her stomach and tried to look ill.

"So go barf and then get back to work," Roxanne said. "If you die, we'll call an ambulance." She hobbled out of the cubicle.

"So much for that idea," Karma said. She looked at her watch. "We can probably get out of here in an hour or so for lunch. We'll just have to go right back to the apartment, and see if Lisha is there."

"But what if she isn't?" Chelsea asked. "What do we do then?"

No one had an answer.

"I know it's not the finest of accommodations," Harley said as he prodded Lisha into the small basement apartment. "My friend is a little low on funds at the moment."

With one hand on the steering wheel and an eye glued on Lisha—he'd tied her hands with a bandanna so she wouldn't try to jump out of the moving car—he had driven them to Alphabet City, east of the East Village, and parked the car on a street with mostly abandoned, deserted buildings.

Then he had walked with Lisha, the hard object still embedded in her spine, to an ancient brown building in the center of the block, and forced her down a flight of steps to this apartment.

Lisha looked around. It was tiny, and filthy, with a threadbare couch, a small TV set, and a card table with a scale on it, and some lengths of rope. Cockroaches crawled over the top of some pizza remains on the floor.

"Make yourself comfortable, Lisha," Harley said, motioning her toward the couch. "I got us a bottle of wine." He opened the grimy refrigerator and took out a bottle of white wine.

"I don't want any." Lisha stood near the couch, her arms wrapped tightly around herself.

"Oh yeah, you do," Harley said. "I remember how much you like to party, baby."

Still watching Lisha intently, he got two cracked

glasses out of a cupboard and poured them each a glass of wine. Then he handed one to Lisha.

"I can't drink it," she said.

"Drink it!" Harley thundered. *"I say you'll drink it and you'll drink it!"*

Lisha put the glass to her lips.

"That's better." Harley's voice returned to normal. "Let's sit on the couch together."

Lisha sat down, a spring from the ancient couch pushing into her thigh. Harley sat next to her, so close that their legs were touching. He put his arm around her.

"Remember when we used to sit like this?" he asked dreamily.

"Uh-huh," Lisha said cautiously.

"We really had a great time together, didn't we?" Harley asked. "You were so crazy about me. You couldn't get enough of me. Remember?"

She nodded her head yes.

"Do you still feel that way, Lish? I really need to know. I mean, I risked a lot to come find you. And I need to know that you appreciate it."

"I . . . do," Lisha managed to lie.

"But see, here's the thing," Harley said, taking a sip of his wine. "You don't act like you appreciate it."

"But I do," she said quickly.

"Yeah?" he asked hopefully. "Prove it to me, baby."

Please, God, please . . .

"Just sitting here like this proves it, doesn't it?" Lisha asked.

"I don't know," Harley said. "I'm afraid maybe you're only here because I forced you." He took another sip of his wine. "Is that true?"

"No," Lisha lied. "I . . . I want to be with you."

"Yeah?" he asked again. "Like how we used to be?"

"Ri-right," she said faintly.

"Well, you never used to sit around with me with so much clothes on," Harley said.

No, no, please.

"I think you should take them off," he said, his tone conversational.

Lisha's eyes flitted to the door, the window, any possible avenue of escape. But the window was tiny, below street level, and obscured by overflowing garbage cans. And Harley had locked the door.

"Take off your clothes, Lisha," he said, his tone dark and threatening.

"I . . . it's really filthy in here, Harley," Lisha said. "I don't want to sit around in here naked."

"Down to your underwear, then," Harley said. "I always did like the way you looked in them."

She hesitated, but the strange, hard, crazy look on his face convinced her.

Slowly, she reached down and pulled the over-sized men's white T-shirt she was wearing over her head. And then she tugged the black Lycra biker shorts off.

She stood before him in a floral-print bra and matching panties.

It's not any skimpier than a bathing suit, she told herself so that she wouldn't fall over from fear. *I have to stay alert. I have to figure out a way to save myself.*

"Cute," Harley said. "Now, come and sit on my lap."

No. I won't do it, Lisha thought. *But I want to live. Would he really kill me? Please, God, I don't know what to do.*

"I have some really romantic plans for us, Lisha. But you know what? You can't have the romance without the finance. Isn't that a good one?"

She managed a smile.

"I heard some dude on a talk show say that," he said, laughing. He looked at his watch. "I need to go make a pickup."

He took her arm and led her to a wooden chair. "Have a seat." Lisha sat. "Put your arms behind you." She did.

Harley picked up one of the ropes from the card table and tied her hands behind her back, around the back of the chair.

"What are you doing?" she asked fearfully.

"What does it look like I'm doing?" he asked. He got another rope and tied her feet to the legs of the chair.

"But . . . but I thought we were going to be together," Lisha said desperately. "Why are you tying me up?"

"So I can go pick up my finance," Harley said. "I thought I just explained that. "This dude owes me some money. And some happy pills. I'll only be gone a little while, baby. Will you miss me?"

127

Maybe if he leaves I can try to escape, she thought. *Maybe it's the only chance I have.*

"I'll miss you," Lisha assured him.

"I knew you would," Harley said. "And when I come back, I'll drop some of my special little happy pills on you. You won't believe how good they make you feel, Lish. I feel like I'm completely alive, for the first time, ever."

He knelt down in front of her and stared into her eyes. His glittered oddly, and a horrible, terrifying thought hit Lisha in the pit of her stomach:

He's completely insane.

"Bye, baby," Harley said. "When I come back, I'll have a big surprise for you." He softly kissed her lips. Then he left, locking the door behind him.

9

"**I**t's twelve o'clock," Chelsea said, pulling off her headset. They had been in Sicko Central, transcribing tapes, with one eye on the clock. The minutes ticked by with agonizing slowness. Every ten minutes they called the apartment again. But Lisha never picked up.

"Let's get out of here," Karma said, grabbing her purse.

"I'm coming with you," Alan insisted.

"Hello, group," Winston said, sticking his head in the door of Sicko Central. "Did Lisha get back from her appointment? I thought I could redeem myself and take her to lunch."

"When did she tell you she had an appointment?" Chelsea demanded.

"This mornin'," Winston answered. "I ran into her in the lobby. Why?"

"Let's go," Karma said.

"Are you going to see Lisha?" Winston asked as the three of them hurried past him. "Tell her I owe her one, mon!"

"She isn't going to be at the apartment," Chelsea said as they practically ran down the hallway to the elevator. "Y'all know that."

"Well, if she's not there we have to go to—" Alan began.

"Interns!" Bigfoot yelled, hobbling toward them on her crutches. "Just where do you think you're going?"

"It's called lunch," Chelsea snapped, so concerned about Lisha that she forgot to use her usual measured tones with her boss.

"No, it's called *working* lunch," Roxanne contradicted. "I need the three of you in my office. Pronto."

"But . . . we have plans we can't get out of," Karma invented.

"Do they involve *Trash*?" Roxanne asked.

"No, but—"

"Then you don't have plans, do you," Roxanne pointed out dismissively. "You can order sandwiches in." She hobbled away from them.

"I truly loathe and despise her." Chelsea was fuming.

"Bigfoot can shove it," Alan said fiercely. "I'm going to the apartment to check on Lisha. If Roxanne wants to fire me, she can fire me."

"Hey, you guys heading out to lunch?" Sky said, walking toward them. "I've got my mind wrapped

130

around a huge pastrami sandwich from Zabar's, how about it?"

"Bigfoot just ordered us to eat in her office," Chelsea explained.

"Tell Roxanne I'll be back as soon as I check on Lisha—" Alan began.

"Check on Lisha for what?" Sky asked.

"It's a long story," Karma said.

"Wait, I have an idea," Chelsea said quickly. "Let Sky go check on Lisha. That way you won't risk your job, Alan."

"I repeat, check on Lisha for what?" Sky said confused.

"See if she's back at our apartment," Chelsea said, fishing her apartment keys out of her backpack and handing them to Sky. "She told Sumtimes she went home sick, but she hasn't answered the phone, and we're worried about her."

"Look, I said I'll go," Alan began.

"No problem," Sky said. "I'm there."

"If she's not there, call us right away and let us know," Alan urged him.

Sky took in their worried faces. "Hey, why do I have the feeling there's more going on here than I know about?"

"Just go," Karma told him.

"Is Lish in some kind of trouble?" Sky asked, clearly concerned.

"If she was, she'd tell me, not you," Alan said brusquely.

"What makes you think so?" Sky asked coldly.

"You guys, this is not the time to pull your macho

crap about Lisha, okay?" Karma said in exasperation. "Just go, Sky!"

"And call us," Chelsea called after him.

All they could do was go to Bigfoot's office.

And wait.

Sweat poured down Lisha's face, mixing with her tears. She didn't know how long it had been since Harley left, since there was no clock in the room. She had tried and tried to free her hands, or her feet, or to move the chair close enough to the window so that she could try to butt her head into it. But all that she had accomplished was to chafe her wrists and ankles so hard against the rope that they burned.

"Somebody! Anybody!" Lisha screamed as loudly as she could. Her throat felt as raw as her wrists and ankles, she had screamed in vain so many times.

"Somebody! Please! Help me!" she screamed again. The tears coursed down her cheeks as sobs were torn from her throat.

Why didn't I do something about Harley a long time ago? Lisha thought in despair. *Why was I so stupid? Oh, God, please, don't punish me because I was so stupid. I'll do anything . . . .*

"Somebody!" she yelled again between her sobs. "Help!"

A key turned in the lock. Lisha held her breath. Harley.

"Why did you do that?" he asked, his voice dangerously soft. "I heard you when I was opening the door."

" Be-because I'm scared," Lisha said.

"Why?" Harley asked.

"Because you kidnapped me and tied me to a chair!" Lisha screamed, crying again.

"If you treated me better, Lish, I wouldn't have to do these things. It's your own fault."

"Please, Harley, untie me," Lisha begged.

"Well, since you asked so nicely." Harley took out his pocketknife and cut through the ropes that held her hands, then her feet.

Lisha sprang to her feet, and stumbled, as the circulation had been cut off in her legs.

"Oopsie," Harley said, righting her. "Come on and sit with me on the couch, Lish. I've got great news."

He held her upper arm in a viselike grip and forced her over to the couch. They sat. "I got money and I got everything we need!"

"For what?" Lisha asked.

Harley looked at her as if she should know the answer to that question. "Our honeymoon, of course!"

He's totally insane. He could do anything. I see that now.

"It's kind of like that *Romeo and Juliet* story, you know?" Harley asked. "They were totally in love. And they were willing to die for it." He stared intensely at Lisha. "That's how much I love you, Lish. Don't you think you should be willing to die for love?"

Lisha hesitated. At that moment the lock turned in the door, and the door opened. Harley jumped up from the couch as a skinny, young guy with bad skin sauntered into the living room.

"What the hell are you doing here, man?" the skinny guy asked.

"Just hanging with my lady, bro," Harley said.

The skinny guy took in Harley's crazed face. "Get the hell outta here. I told you not to come here anymore. I didn't even know you still had a key."

"Hey, chill out," Harley said. "I'm just kickin' it, you know."

"You ain't kickin' it, fool," the skinny guy spat. "You got a chick in here in her underwear, and you're way high, man. Don't mess with me, Harley."

"You shouldn't be talking to me that way," Harley said, scowling.

"I told you, man, I don't want you around here anymore. You're friggin' crazy. A lunatic. You're stupid enough to take them pills and mess yourself up, it ain't my problem. Now get the hell outta here, I got business to do here."

Harley raised his right hand. The one with the weapon in it.

"Don't even think about it, man," the skinny guy said with disgust. "You waste me, the big guys will be all over you, and you'll wish you were dead way before your heart stops beating. Now get the hell outta here, Harley. I mean it."

"Please call the police—" Lisha cried, running over to the skinny guy.

"Yeah, right," the skinny guy snorted. "I don't know who the hell you are and I don't wanna know."

"I'm—" Lisha began.

"Hey, shut up!" the guy yelled. "I ain't gettin' involved! Now, both of you, get the hell outta here."

"Please!" Lisha yelled desperately. "He's going to kill me!"

"He's a wuss, he ain't gonna kill you." The skinny guy swiped his hand over his buzz-cut hair and sat at the table. "I mean, the dude is psycho, but he's still a wuss."

"Let's go, Lisha," Harley said, "This place isn't good enough for us, anyway."

Lisha reached for her clothes.

"Uh uh," Harley said. "Leave 'em."

"But—"

"Just the T-shirt. Move!" Harley repeated, his voice tight. Lisha quickly pulled the T-shirt over her head

"Let's go."

He grabbed a length of the rope, and then pushed Lisha across the room and out the front door.

"You lied to me, Lisha," he said from behind her, his voice low in her hair.

"No, I—"

"You lied," Harley said dangerously. "You didn't really come with me because you love me. You came because I made you."

"Maybe if we could just go someplace and talk, we—"

"Yeah, right," Harley snorted. "Now that I see

your true colors? What do you think I am, stupid? We're going for another ride, Lisha."

She gulped hard. "Where to?"

"Someplace where no one will find us," Harley said.

He prodded her toward the car. Two young boys zoomed by on their bikes, but they didn't seem to take any notice of the fact that Lisha was wearing nothing but a long T-shirt.

Maybe I should try and make a run for it, she thought. *That guy in there said Harley would never shoot me. But what if he's wrong? I don't know what to do!*

They had reached the car. Lisha reached for the door.

"No," Harley said quickly, and he prodded her around to the back of the car.

"What?" she asked fearfully.

"I hate to do this to you, Lisha, but I can't trust you anymore." His eyes slid significantly to the trunk of the car. "You have to travel in the trunk."

"No!" Lisha yelled, and she looked desperately down the block to see if there was someone, anyone, who could help her.

It was deserted.

"In," Harley ordered, opening the trunk.

"No, please—"

Harley turned Lisha around and gave her a crazed smile, and nodded his head toward the trunk.

She climbed in. He slammed it shut.

And then, there was only darkness.

"Yeah, like this makes sense," Karma said, putting yet another credit-card carbon into the pile accumulating in front of her. "We had to stay in for lunch to file credit-card receipts."

Chelsea separated two copies of a Visa bill and put them into the appropriate piles. She kept looking over at Bigfoot's phone.

"I wish Sky would just call, already," she said anxiously.

"You know Lisha's not going to be home," Alan said flatly.

"We don't know anything yet," Chelsea disagreed halfheartedly.

"Your gut is speaking to you, big time, and so is mine," Alan insisted. "We can't mess around with this! We're going to have to go to the police!"

"Yeah, but what if it turns out to be some totally

innocent thing?" Karma's voice was filled with worry. "Lisha would kill us if we went to the police."

"What if it turns out to be this crazy ex-boyfriend with the gun?" Alan challenged. "Are you really willing to risk Lisha's life just so she won't be ticked off at you?"

"How many?" Sumtimes asked, sticking her head in the door.

"We lost count," Alan replied, scowling as he pulled apart another set of receipts. "A lot."

"Good," Sumtimes said. "Hey, Roxanne told me you guys volunteered to stay in for lunch to do this. Thanks. You want to order lunch up?"

"We're not hungry," Chelsea said.

"Oh, well, if you get hungry, use Roxanne's phone to order out. Charge it to *Trash.*" She smiled and left.

Chelsea stared at the phone again. "Ring!" she commanded it. "Ring right now!"

As if on cue, the phone rang, startling them all so much, they nearly jumped out of their seats.

Chelsea picked up the phone. "Roxanne Renault's office," she said. "Chelsea Jennings, intern, speaking."

"Yeah, it's me," Sky said. "I'm at your apartment, and she's not here."

"Is it Sky?" Karma asked hopefully.

Chelsea nodded. "Is there any sign that she's been there at all?" she asked Sky.

"None that I can see," he told her. "I checked your answering machine, and other than a whole lot of calls from you, and a message from Lydia Love from *Rave,* there was nothing at all."

"What's he saying?" Alan demanded.

"He says there's no sign of her," Chelsea told Alan.

"Chels," Sky said urgently into the phone, "what the hell is going on?"

"Come on back here," she said, "and . . . and I'll tell you," she decided. "You might as well get Nick and Demetrius, too. We can all try to figure out what to do together." Chelsea hung up.

"Are you sure that's the right thing to do?" Karma asked.

"No," Chelsea admitted. "The only thing I'm sure of is that I'm scared. Really scared. Like deep-in-the-pit-of-my-stomach scared."

She closed her eyes and an image of Lisha, with her bangs in her eyes, her hands on her hips, flashed into her mind.

And then she saw another image of Lisha, back when she was still little Alyssa Bishop, Chelsea's very best friend. Feisty. Strong-willed. Funny. And tougher than anyone that Chelsea knew.

I know you're in danger, Lisha. I feel it.

"You think Harley has her, don't you," Alan said, crossing the room to take Chelsea's hand.

Chelsea nodded, too scared to even speak.

She closed her eyes again. *Wherever you are, Lisha, you have to fight. Do you hear me? You have to fight back! You can't give up now. We love you.*

Now, fight back!

*　　*　　*

I have to stay alert, I have to keep breathing, Lisha thought as the car bumped along the road. It was totally dark in the trunk, and she could feel herself hyperventilating from fear. Right before she'd gotten into the trunk, Harley had tied her hands with the piece of rope he'd brought from the apartment, and slipped his red bandanna over her mouth, tying it behind her head. The bandanna made it difficult to breathe through her mouth at all, and the rope cut into her already tender and bleeding wrists.

Breathe deeply, she told herself. *Keep taking long, slow breaths.*

The air was so thin in the trunk, she felt as if she was suffocating. Sweat poured down her face, stinging her eyes. She was folded into a fetal position, her feet tucked under her.

"Ugh," she grunted as the car went over a huge pothole. Her head bounced against the top of the trunk.

Breathe. Keep breathing. Through your nose. That's it. Keep thinking. You have to save yourself. You have to live.

She felt the car speed up, and then the ride got smoother.

The FDR, she thought. *Or maybe the West Side Highway. Less potholes than the streets. Where is he taking me?*

Beep! Beep-beep-beep!

The car slowed down abruptly, and Lisha heard cars honking all around her.

A traffic jam. Wherever we are, there's a traffic jam.

Honk! Honk-honk-ho-o-o-o-nk!

Now more cars were sounding off.

A thought flashed through her head. Something she had seen on a talk show. Something about what to do if you were ever abducted and stuck in the trunk of a car.

And I thought it was such a stupid show at the time, Lisha recalled. *Just designed to scare people and get ratings. What did that expert say? He said to do anything to attract attention to the car. But what? What was it?*

I remember! He said if you kicked the taillight hard enough from inside the trunk, you could kick it out. A busted taillight might attract the police. And it would also let more air into the trunk so that I can breathe.

Honk-honk-ho-o-o-onk!

The car was still not moving, stuck somewhere.

The cars honking will muffle any noise I make, Lisha thought. *Harley won't know to get suspicious. If I can only turn over and try to kick out the taillight.*

Lisha tried to turn her body, but the space was so small that she was stuck in her position, on her side. She tried to kick backward, with her heel, toward the light, but her efforts were awkward and ineffectual.

Come on, Lisha, she told herself. *You have to find a way to do this. You have to try to save your own life.*

Slowly, grunting with the effort, little by little, she managed to edge her body onto her back.

Thank you, God, thank you, she prayed. Her breaths were rapid and shallow now. There was barely enough air in the trunk for her to breathe at all. Sweat dripped into her eyes, her mouth. She felt light-headed, faint, dizzy, and nauseous.

You can't pass out, she told herself. *You have to fight. Fight!*

But she could feel the lack of oxygen dragging her down, down to some place where all the fear went away, where she never had to see Harley again, or be afraid, or be ashamed about everything that had happened in Europe.

It would be so easy to just give up, give in, Lisha thought dreamily. She closed her eyes. *You'll never have to face any of the bad stuff ever again. You can just sleep.*

Chelsea.

Chelsea's face sprang into her mind. It was almost as if she could hear her old friend calling to her, willing her to stay awake, to try, to fight.

Lisha's eyes sprang open.

Fight! Fight, dammit!

Lisha forced her mind to concentrate. Everything felt so fuzzy, out of focus.

What was I trying to do? The taillight. Right. Kick out the taillight.

Just do it. This may be the only chance you have, she told herself. Lisha willed herself to stay awake and alert. She bit her own lips, hard, just to jar herself.

You still have your cowboy boots on, Lish, she told herself. *And just think, you hardly ever wear them anymore. Thank God Harley didn't make you take off those when he made you strip.*

She got angry all over again when she thought of how demeaning that had been. *Anger is good,* she told herself. *Get pissed off.*

And save your life.

She raised her knee as best she could in the cramped space, and aimed for where she thought the inside of the light would be.

She hit metal. Hard.

Try again, Lisha, she told herself, panting now from fear, exertion, heat, and lack of oxygen. *You have to find the strength to try again.*

She lifted her booted foot again, and aimed, farther to the right this time.

She hit something, not metal, something smoother, a different surface.

Glass.

The inside of the light. Maybe even the brake light. Or the turn signal.

Honk, honk, ho-o-o-o-nk!

She lifted her foot again, and jammed it as hard as she could at what she hoped was the same spot. Yes! She felt a splintering, and quickly she jammed her foot into it again, and again.

Daylight! She could see daylight coming in from where the light had been! Lisha took huge gulps of fresh air, drinking it in hungrily.

The car began to move, picking up speed quickly. Lisha was able to see through the hole where the taillight had been, but all she could make out was the edge of a car or the wheels of a truck.

143

They traveled for a long time, Lisha staying alert, trying to catch anything through the tiny spot into the outside world that might give her a clue, might help her save her life.

The car rolled to a stop. Where were they? She could feel that the motor was still running. She tried her best to see out of the busted taillight. There was another car just behind them. But even though neither car was moving, this time no one honked their horn.

Now the car moved forward a little, then stopped again.

A tollbooth! Lisha thought. *That could be it! We could be at a tollbooth. That means we're leaving Manhattan.*

The car rolled forward, then stopped yet again. Now the car moved again, not too fast, but it didn't stop again.

If only I could scream! Lisha thought desperately. She tried to make some sounds around the bandanna, but all that came out was a puny, muffled sound.

The car sped up, and she tried frantically to think of something, anything else she could do. When the car slowed down again, as if they were once again in some traffic, an idea flew into her mind.

Rock the car, she thought. *I've got to try to rock the car while it's standing still.*

Using all her strength, she threw her body forward, then backward, over and over. She moved as much as she could, grunting from the exertion.

The car started up again, and Lisha felt Harley switch lanes, and then put on a burst of speed. A good burst of speed.

No one saw, Lisha thought despairingly. *And no one is going to see the busted light, either. Probably the only thing I accomplished is that I made Harley mad for rocking the car that way. And I don't know what he'll do to me if he's mad. What if he—*

"Pull over into the right lane," came a loud authoritative voice through a megaphone.

The car sped up.

"Brown Ford Mustang, pull over to the right immediately. I repeat, pull over immediately!"

Oh, my God, that's this car! Lisha realized. *And that must be the police! Please, God, please, let me be saved. Please, don't let anyone shoot anyone.*

Lisha felt the car swerve to the right, then slow down, then stop. Harley turned off the motor.

She did her best to scream around the bandanna. She rocked the car as hard as she could, flinging herself around the trunk.

"New York Police Department," Lisha heard a deep, masculine voice say. "You're speeding, mister. And you've got a broken taillight. Please step out of the car, sir."

Lisha felt Harley's weight leave the car. "What's up, Officers?" she heard him yell as he closed his door.

"What is in your trunk, sir?"

"Nothing!" Harley said.

Lisha tried to scream again. She rocked the car.

"Step to the side of the car and put your hands on the hood," she heard the cop say over his loudspeaker.

"Hey!" the cop yelled. "Drop the—what do you think you're doing? Hey!"

And Lisha heard a shot. And then another.

Oh, no, she thought. *They're shooting at each other.*

And then there was no more shooting.

He's dead, Lisha thought. *Or the cops are dead. Or—*

A few moments later the trunk was being pried open. It was one of the policemen, an older black man with a kindly face.

"Sweet Lord," he said as he looked down at Lisha. He reached in and pulled her up, and then lifted her out of the trunk.

"Where's Harley?" she tried to ask, but her voice was still muffled by the bandanna.

The cop pulled the bandanna free.

"Where's Harley?" Lisha repeated.

The cop pointed to the railing of the bridge, which Lisha knew spanned the confluence of the Hudson River and the East River, just as more police cars were arriving.

"Miss, he jumped, miss," the cop said.

Gently, he untied her hands.

"He jumped?"

"Are you okay, miss?"

"Yes," Lisha said shakily, tears of relief falling down her face.

146

"Do you know this man?" the older cop asked.

"Yes," Lisha said, fisting the tears off her cheeks. Cars were going by at a snail's pace, everyone staring at her, gawking. She turned back to the older cop. "His name is Harley McCloud. He's been stalking me. He abducted me from work.

"He has a gun, somewhere," she added.

"He used it," the cop told her. "But he missed."

"Thank God," Lisha said.

"It's a long way to the river," the cop observed to Lisha. "I don't think you have to worry about this guy Harley stalking you ever again."

Chelsea and Karma hurried up the walkway to the downtown headquarters of the New York Police Department.

Chelsea had received a call from Lisha about one o'clock, and the call had been transferred to Bigfoot's office. Sky was back, and the group was just on the verge of calling the police when Lisha called from the police station.

All she had told them was to please bring her some shorts, and to come and get her. Chelsea had begged Sumtimes—their only boss who ever revealed a trace of humanity—to let her and Karma go. Something in the desperation of her voice seemed to make Sumtimes say yes.

They had hopped into a taxi, and Karma waited in front of their apartment while Chelsea hurried upstairs and grabbed a pair of shorts for Lisha, then they sped downtown. For once, traffic was relatively light.

Lisha had told Chelsea almost nothing about what had happened. Or why she needed shorts. Or why she was at police headquarters.

The only thing she said was that it had to do with Harley, and then she started crying so hard she couldn't speak.

"Can I help you?" the female officer behind the front desk at reception area asked Chelsea and Karma.

"Yes, we're here for our friend Lisha Bishop," Chelsea said.

"Your names?" the officer asked.

They gave their names.

The officer scanned a printout on a clipboard, then she called someone, gave some information, and hung up again. "Miss Bishop is waiting for you in Room two," the officer said. "Down the corridor, second door on the right."

"Thank you," Chelsea said.

They hurried down the corridor, and opened the door marked "2."

Lisha was sitting in a wooden chair, her head in her hands.

She was wearing the jacket to a police officer's uniform over a T-shirt and her floral-print underwear.

"Lisha!" Chelsea cried.

She and Karma ran to their friend, and the three of them embraced. Lisha rested her head on

Chelsea's shoulder. She didn't cry. When she looked up, Chelsea handed her the shorts.

"What happened?" Karma asked anxiously.

"We were so worried about you," Chelsea added.

Lisha finished dressing and sat down with her two friends. "You could say that today was the worst day of my entire life," she said shakily.

Chelsea and Karma waited.

And then slowly, painfully, Lisha told them everything that had happened, ending with Harley's high dive into the murky water.

"Do they—do they think he's dead?" Chelsea asked, wide-eyed.

Lisha nodded. "I guess they wait to see if a body ever floats up. But the police didn't seem to think he could live after falling that far. And no body surfaced that they could see. They've been checking."

"Oh, my God," Chelsea breathed, her hand to her mouth. "Oh, Lish . . ."

"I just . . . I feel like I'm having some terrible nightmare, you know?" Lisha said. "I keep thinking I'll wake up—"

"At least you know he can't hurt you anymore," Karma said gently.

"If he's dead, he can't," Lisha said. "But what if he isn't?" Tears came to her eyes. "And what if he is? Is it my fault?"

"No, no, of course not!" Chelsea exclaimed. "He was sick! And crazy! He did it himself!"

"He could have killed you, Lish," Karma added.

Lisha wiped the tears from her eyes. "I keep thinking about what that guy said in the apartment.

151

That Harley would never really use his gun. He was right, sort of. He didn't use it on me."

"But you had no way of knowing if he really would or not," Chelsea reminded her.

Lisha's eyes filled with tears again. "I loved him once," she said. "Or at least I thought I did."

"Can we take you home?" Chelsea asked her.

Lisha nodded. "I just have to sign some papers. I gave the police a statement already. Some detective said he'd be calling me soon."

"They don't know anything about . . . the thing in Europe, do they?" Chelsea asked carefully.

"Only that Harley was my boyfriend back then," Lisha said. "And that he was a drug dealer. Nothing else."

"So, you really *are* free now," Karma said. "You know what I mean."

"Yeah," Lisha said. "I'm really free." Her eyes filled with tears again. "And all I feel is really, really sad."

"You want more, Lish?" Alan asked, holding the white carton of noodles with sesame paste over Lisha's dish.

"No, thanks," Lisha said.

"How about some rice?" Sky offered.

"No, I'm full, honest," Lisha replied.

It was later that evening, and the six interns were gathered at the girls' apartment, eating Chinese food they had ordered in. Demetrius was working late, but he was supposed to come over later. The girls had filled the guys in on everything that had happened to Lisha, and everyone was being very solicitous of her feelings.

"You hot or cold or anything?" Chelsea asked.

"Want Belch to do a trick for you?" Nick offered. Belch wagged his tail violently at the mention of his name, and Nick scratched the little dog behind his ears. "Belch can cheer up anyone."

"You guys, I'm not an invalid," Lisha said. "I'm okay."

"Well, I wouldn't be if what happened to you today happened to me," Chelsea said, shaking her head. "I'd be a wreck."

"What's the point?" Lisha asked.

"See, when most people are, like, losing it, they're too upset to ask 'what's the point?'" Karma explained.

"I'm not most people, then," Lisha replied, shaking her bangs out of her eyes.

"Supergirl, that's you, Lish," Sky said. "Nothing gets to you."

Lisha shrugged, but she couldn't look at him. *You get to me,* she wanted to say. *I wish I could just cry in your arms. But it's too scary. And I refuse to be that weak.*

"At least something good came out of all of this," Nick said. "Now we know who took the film from the Trash-cam."

"You really think Winston won't turn us in?" Sky asked Lisha dubiously.

"He said he wouldn't," Lisha said.

Nick fed Belch a piece of shrimp. "And Winston

153

planned all the woo-woo stuff just to get you to go out with him?"

"He thought he was being clever," Karma said, getting up to pour herself a cup of coffee. "And I supposed if all this weirdness with Harley hadn't been going on, it might have been kinda funny."

"He seems like a nice guy," Alan offered.

"Too many guys want you, Lish," Sky said, his voice a little too hearty. "How are you ever gonna choose?"

"I'm not, okay?" Lisha snapped.

"Hey, don't bite my head off," Sky said. "It's not my fault if you're irresistible."

"Look, I don't need to hear that right now, okay?" Lisha said sharply. She got up and strode to her room. From behind her, she could hear Sky asking the others, "What did I say?" but she slammed her bedroom door shut before she heard anyone's answer.

Lisha threw herself on her water bed and stared up at the ceiling. *I want to cry, but I can't,* she realized. *It's like there's this huge lump of pain, and it's blocking my tears. And I can't let myself . . . I just can't let myself.*

There was a soft knock on her door.

"Who is it?" Lisha asked.

"Alan."

She got up and opened the door. Alan stepped into her room. Then he closed the door behind him. Lisha returned to the water bed. Alan sat on the edge. They didn't speak.

Then slowly, wordlessly, Alan lay down next to

her. He opened his arms. And Lisha moved her head to the comfort of his shoulder. His arms circled her, and the water bed gently rippled underneath them.

Then the tears began to fall. Alan didn't make her talk, or say anything himself, he just held her, and let her cry.

"No, no, don't!" Lisha screamed, fighting Harley off. He was reaching for her, his hands wrapped around her neck. She managed to feint out of his grasp, and then she was falling backward, into the water, falling, and she couldn't breathe, couldn't breathe, couldn't—"

"Lish? Lish, honey?" Alan said softly. "Wake up. You're having a nightmare."

Lisha opened her eyes. Moonlight streamed in through the window, illuminating Alan's beautiful, kind, dark eyes.

"It was so horrible," Lisha whispered. "Harley was strangling me. And then I jumped, and I was drowning. . . ."

"He put his arms around her. "It's okay," he said. "You're safe. I'm right here."

She breathed in the comfort of him, burrowing into his embrace. When she could feel her heartbeat returning to normal, she kissed his cheek. "What time is it?" she whispered.

He looked at the hands of his luminous watch. "Three o'clock."

"In the morning?" Lisha asked, shocked.

"You slept," Alan said.

155

"I can't believe I slept for so long. Have you been awake all this time?" she asked.

"Watching you," Alan answered.

"Watching over me is more like it," Lisha said, touched by his caring. "You didn't have to."

"I know."

"I'm really okay," she insisted.

"I know."

Her lips trembled as tears sprang to her eyes again. "That's a big, fat lie," she said.

"I know that, too." He wrapped her in his arms again.

"How did you get so sweet?" Lisha asked, when she managed to stop crying again.

"Let's see, must have been all those protests against my macho dad," Alan said, a half smile on his lips.

"He's lucky to have you for a son," Lisha said fervently.

"I'll tell him you said so," Alan said wryly. "That is, if the two of us ever have an actual conversation."

Lisha rolled over and reached for some Kleenex on her nightstand. "Life is so crazy, Alan. I really don't get it at all." She blew her nose hard. "There was a time when I really, really thought I loved Harley. And now he's . . . he's . . ." She couldn't bring herself to say it.

"But the guy that died today isn't the guy you loved," Alan pointed out.

"Who was he, then? I mean, why did I think I loved him? What is love, anyway?"

"The greatest writers in the world have tackled that one," Alan said. "I'm out of my league. Hell, I can't even get past page fifty of my novel."

"Are you ever going to let me read what you're writing?" Lisha asked.

"Maybe someday. If I ever think it's any good." He stroked her hair softly.

"Well, I know one thing," Lisha said. "Love is stupid. It hurts. It makes your life crazy. And it's not worth the pain and trouble."

"That's how you feel now, Lish. But it's not forever," Alan said gently.

"Yes, it is," she insisted. "And another thing. Lust. I mean, just because you want to jump someone's bones doesn't make it love. It's just some stupid physical thing, and people make it something it isn't."

"Like you and Sky?" Alan asked softly.

"I don't love Sky!" Lisha denied sharply.

"It's okay if you do, Lish—"

"I don't," Lisha stated firmly.

"You want him, though," Alan said, his voice low.

"No."

Alan didn't say anything, he just held her.

Lisha got up on one elbow and looked into Alan's eyes. "No one makes me feel the way you do, Alan. Safe. Peaceful."

"But no fire," Alan said. He smiled a small, sad smile. "Someone else told me that once."

"I never said there was no fire," Lisha whispered. Then she leaned down, and softly, slowly, she

157

kissed his lips. Then she kissed him again, until his arms tightened around her, and he began to return her kisses passionately.

And finally, after they got lost in the sweetness and heat of each other, as dawn was coming up outside their window, Lisha fell asleep, safe in Alan's arms.

"Alan!" Karma said, when Alan padded into the kitchen later that morning. "Hi!"

"Hi," Alan responded. He found his sneakers under the couch and put them on.

Karma was dressed for work, in a black-and-white Betsy Johnson, geometric print, op-art shift from the sixties, with chunky white high-heeled loafers. Her hair was in a fat braid that started high on her head and flowed down her back.

"So . . . you spent the night with Lisha," Karma said brightly, pouring coffee from the Mr. Coffee.

Alan didn't reply; he just tied his shoes.

"So, do you want coffee?"

"Nah, I'm gonna go catch a quick shower before work," he said. "Thanks, though." He slipped out the front door.

Lisha came into the living room, her hair tousled from sleep, clad in a T-shirt and panties. "Where's Alan?"

"He went across the hall to take a shower," Karma said, sipping her coffee. "He was here the whole night, huh."

"Huh," Lisha agreed, pouring herself a cup of coffee.

158

"Oh," Karma said. "I'm dying of curiosity, of course, but I'm much too discreet to ask you anything."

Lisha got the milk out of the refrigerator and poured some into her coffee.

"The gossip of the morning, besides you and Alan, is that Chelsea spent the night across the hall with Nick. Demetrius never made it over here last night. Which means that I'm the only one who slept alone."

"What time is it?" Lisha asked, stirring her coffee.

"Eight," Karma answered. "How are you feeling?"

"Better," Lisha said. "I mean, I still have a ways to go. And the whole thing was just so horrible, but . . . better." She sipped her coffee.

"Alan helped, huh?" Karma asked.

"Yeah," Lisha replied.

"Like, how did he help?" Karma reached into the brown bag on the counter for a bagel.

"Just by being Alan," Lisha said.

"Uh-huh," Karma murmured. "Is that as in friend-Alan, or as in lover-Alan?"

"Lover," Lisha mused. "What an old-fashioned word. You don't hear that word much anymore, huh?"

"Because it's, like, out of some romance novel," Karma said. "You know, the ones with the cover where some hunky guy is holding some girl with her clothes falling off. And speaking of clothes falling off—"

Lisha plopped down in the chair in the living room. "What?"

"You're not wearing much," Karma noted.

"That's because I didn't get dressed yet," Lisha said.

"Yeah," Karma agreed. "I was wondering if you had ever gotten *un*dressed." She got the cream cheese out of the refrigerator and spread it on her bagel.

"You're trying to find out if I made love with Alan, aren't you?" Lisha said calmly, sipping her coffee.

"Would I do that?" Karma whined. She brought her bagel into the living room and sat on the couch. "Now, tell me every steamy detail."

"Well, it was nice," Lisha said.

"There are many kinds of nice," Karma pointed out.

"Alan is . . . well, he's really special," Lisha said dreamily.

"I know that," Karma said. "I love him like a brother. The question is, do you love him like a brother?"

"No," Lisha said.

"No?"

"No," Lisha confirmed.

"You mean you . . . but I thought you and Sky . . ."

"Okay, okay, I'm attracted to Sky," Lisha admitted. "But that's just my body. My heart says . . . Alan."

"Are you sure?" Karma asked.

No, Lisha thought. *That's the truth. I'm not sure. I don't think I've ever been as attracted to anyone as I am to Sky. But I can't handle that now, not after what happened yesterday.*

"Physical attraction isn't everything," she told Karma, sipping her coffee.

"Okay, it's not everything," Karma agreed. "But it's a lot. So, do your knees get weak when Alan holds you? Do you get that funny little feeling in the pit of your stomach when you even think about him?"

"I am definitely attracted to him," Lisha said firmly. "And more than that, I trust him. I've had it with hot guys I can't trust."

"So, did you sleep with him?" Karma asked.

"Yeah," Lisha said.

"Yes? *You did?*" Karma cried.

"He was here all night, we slept—"

"That's not exactly what I meant," Karma said. "Did you—"

"I hate him," Chelsea announced, stomping through the front door.

"Who?" Karma asked.

"Nick." Chelsea slammed the door behind her. "I hate him."

"Didn't you just spend the night with him for the very first time?" Karma asked. "Or did I miss something in the continuing saga of you and Nick?"

"I spent the night with him," Chelsea said. "We didn't have sex. We almost did, but then I thought, 'No, the first time I have sex is not going to be like this. It's going to be really, really special. Nick and

I will rent the most opulent hotel room in New York, and we'll have champagne, and the bed will be strewn with rose petals. . . .'" Tears filled her eyes. "So, last night, I told him I still wanted to wait. And he was so sweet about it. He said he wanted to make it perfect for me, and he'd wait until I was ready. And now I never want to speak to him again as long as I live!"

"I take it you two had a fight," Lisha stated dryly.

"This morning when we woke up," Chelsea said. "It was so wonderful to wake up with him. And then . . . and then he told me . . . Oh, Lish, you were right. Just because you're attracted to someone doesn't make it love. How could I have believed that I love him?"

"What did he do?" Karma asked.

"I don't know, that's just it," Chelsea said. She sat next to Karma on the couch. "You know how Jazz invited Nick to go to the Rock of Ages Awards with her, and how she's been asking him to come into her office, and flirting with him again and everything? Well, now I know why."

"She wants him?" Lisha guessed.

"Worse," Chelsea said. "I think she already had him. Jazz is pregnant."

Karma and Lisha's mouths hung open in disbelief.

"She's—" Karma began.

Chelsea nodded miserably. "He just told me. It's supposed to be this big secret, but he confided in me. He was afraid I'd be upset, he said. People might jump to conclusions, since everyone knows

162

they were dating, and that's why she told him. That's what he *says,* anyway."

"Oh, my God, this really *is* a soap opera!" Karma cried.

Lisha was incredulous. "You mean to tell me that there's a possibility that Jazz is pregnant with Nick's baby?"

"I don't know," Chelsea said. "But I'm going to find out the truth. If it's the last thing I do."

THE TRASH CAN

Dear Readers,

Well, the mail just keeps pouring in. Between the pubbing of *Sunset Forever*, the launch of *Trash*, and my syndicated teen advice column, *Hey, Cherie!*, we've been getting more mail than ever. Hey, Jeff and I are honored, so keep writing!

I wish you guys could see my office. One entire wall is covered, floor to ceiling, with photos of our incredible readers from all over the world. Send us your photo and join the wall! On the opposite wall I have photos of Anne Frank and some other teens and kids who died in the Holocaust. Having the faces of these teens facing my readers across the room, with me in the middle writing, is both inspirational and sobering.

Jeff and I just moved into a new apartment, and he's busy hanging stuff, which is why I'm writing this letter by myself. But of course, Jeff sends his love. And speaking of love, you guys really seem to be loving *Trash*. And we're so glad, because we love it, too! Please send any and all ideas for the series. We want to know.

So, what's coming up for *Trash*, you ask? Well, in *Trash #4: Dirty Big Secrets*, you'll be shocked at what Chelsea finds out about Nick and Jazz! And in *Trash #5: The Evil Twin*, Karma has to decide if blood is thick enough to save her sister's life, even if it means risking her own. *Trash #6: Truth or Scare*, is our most romantic book yet. Lisha has to choose between two guys!

As always, thank you so much for your letters and for your support of our new series. If you have any trouble finding *Trash* at your bookseller, let us know. Send us the name and address of the bookstore and we'll try to help.

And remember, just because we call it *Trash* doesn't make it trash, right?

How TRASHy it is!

Cherie (and Jeff from the other room)

Dear Cherie and Jeff,

I just finished reading the first two *Trash* books and I couldn't put them down. The way you ended them makes me crazy, though. How am I supposed to wait until the next book comes out? I have a question that's kind of personal. Karma's boyfriend, Demetrius, is really tall and Karma is short. Well, I have the opposite problem. My boyfriend is kind of short and I'm two inches taller than he is. He's the nicest guy I ever knew, but I feel self-conscious, like everyone is staring at us. I know it's shallow to feel this way, and I'm not a shallow person, but I can't seem to get over this. What would Chelsea, Karma, or Lisha do if they fell for a short guy?

Melissa Brundi
Waco, Texas

Dear Melissa,

We know those *Trash* cliff-hanger endings can be frustrating, but all you have to do is pick up the next book to know how everything turns out! About the height thing: to be a teenager is to be self-conscious by definition.

Believe us, it gets better! Unless you, say, grow a third eye in the middle of your forehead, everyone is not staring at you. They are too busy worrying about whatever it is that they feel self-conscious about. If this guy is great, be a cool enough person to get over the height issue. If anyone rags on you, they are the small person, not you. Karma, Chelsea, and Lisha definitely agree with that advice!

Dear Cherie and Jeff,

My boyfriend and I are writing this letter to you together to say thank you. We've been together for three years. When we first started dating, I got him to read your *Sunset* books and now we're both reading *Trash*. At first he said no way was he reading a girls' series, but he found out that the problems the girls in your books go through are really similar to the problems we deal with. For example, my boyfriend is adopted, and he found out he has a sister that he never knew about, just like Karma, so *Love, Lies and Video* really helped him. Also, he's Canadian and I'm American, just like Nick and Chelsea. For my birthday, he gave me a puppy and we named him Belch! We would both love to see a story from the guy's point of view. Keep up the great new series. And please get the word out that couples can read your books together, okay?

Kristen Grovnik
Billy Andersen

Dear Kristen and Billy,

What a great letter! Since we're writing this series as a couple it makes sense that couples would want to read it together. You'll find that future *Trash* books are written from both girl and guy points of view. For example, in *Trash #4: Dirty Big Secrets* we get inside Nick's head big-time. Hope that speaks to you, Billy! Any other couples who are reading *Trash* together, write and tell us all about you. We'd love to hear from you.

Dear Cherie and Jeff,

I am totally crazed for *Trash.* I would give anything to be an intern on a TV talk show, even if I did have to shovel dalmatian poop! How do you get a job like that in real life? My dream is to be a TV news reporter one day. I have no idea how to go about it, though. I'm fourteen and I live in a tiny town, but my dreams are huge! Can you help me?

Leeanna Bishop
Flat Rock, North Carolina

Dear Leeanna,

Hey, big dreams are key! If you can't dream it, you can't attain it, right? Of course, along with the dream comes hard work. Here's the plan to achieve your goal. Get great grades and get into the best college you can with a first-rate communications department. Work at the college TV or radio station. You can also volunteer for the local PBS station. Do any low-level job anyone will allow you to do for free, and work your way up. If you're good enough, smart enough, and work hard enough, you'll eventually become indispensable. Then you move up and out from there. Good luck, and go for it!